DEADLY CHEMISTRY

TERI ANNE STANLEY

Entangled Publishing, LLC
2614 South Timberline Road
Suite 109
Fort Collins, CO 80525
Visit our website at www.entangledpublishing.com.

Ignite is an imprint of Entangled Publishing, LLC.

Edited by Rochelle French and Stephen Morgan

Cover design by Fiona Jayde

Manufactured in the United States of America

First Edition June 2014

For Tom, my own personal hero.

Chapter One

Lauren wasn't hoping to find a knight in a shining Tucker University Maintenance uniform when she left her lab at the crack of dawn. She was *hoping* to find the car keys she'd tossed in true absent-minded professor style into the bottom of her bag when she'd been worrying about why her alarm system was malfunctioning, worrying about her project, worrying about getting funding for her project, and worrying about dying in obscurity as a failed scientist in the event a tractor trailer ran the one stop light in the center of town and smushed her—so she didn't see the man who knelt next to the door until she tripped over him.

As she flew ass-over-tea-kettle, he caught her in his— whoa—incredibly, uh, *firm* arms.

She sprawled, half on the concrete, half on the lap of— she looked at the breast pocket of his shirt—*Mike*. Mike The Hottest Maintenance Man In History. But of course, that last part didn't quite fit on his name tag. Dark brown eyes, a chiseled jaw, curly-but-not-girly black hair. There was some-thing edgy and dangerous about him that said, *I'm all man and you'd better watch out*.

She was trying to figure out how to thank him and stand up without making more of a fool of herself when he spoke.

"Are you all right?"

Oh, my.

He had quite the voice. Not quite Darth Vader deep, but damn close. Like that country singer, the one with the bad reputation—low, with a touch of bluegrass twang.

"Oh boy," she murmured.

His lips rose at one corner. "Are you hurt?" He waited, one long, muscular arm stretching around her shoulders to keep the glass door from shutting on her head.

She thought for a second—maybe two—about staying there for a while, next to his Irish Spring and fabric softener-scented self.

"Oh, boy."

"You said that already."

"Okay."

Now the lips were in an official smile.

Oh, hell. "Oh, hell."

Mike The *Smiling* Hot Maintenance Man's expression took on a hint of confusion, jolting Lauren out of her sex-starved, pathetic, crazy cat lady—who'd never been so close to that much testosterone—daze.

"Do you need me to call 911?"

That voice again. It did *stuff* to her...parts. "No, it was just another false alarm." She gathered the few wits she could find and clambered to her feet.

He rose with her, then bent to pick up a pen, a quarter,

and—*lovely*—her tampon case, which had all fallen from her purse when she tripped. He didn't skip a beat, just handed her everything. "What false alarm?"

"Oh. You meant…911 because I fell." Her face heated. Apparently, the spill had jarred a few brain cells loose. "Thanks. I'm okay. The false alarm"—she waved her hand vaguely in the direction of the lab she'd come from—"is from a monitor on a secure cell culture incubator that keeps going off in the middle of the night. There's never anything wrong, but when it goes off, my phone buzzes until I come in and reset it. The alarm. Not my phone." *There.* That was almost coherent.

"I can come by later and see if you've got a bad electrical connection," he said, his forehead—his strong, high forehead—creased in thought.

Geez. When did foreheads get sexy? She really needed to get out of the lab a little more often. "Um, okay." Reaching into her bag and finding her keys on the first grab this time, she said, "That would be great. My lab is 403. Whenever you want to stop by. That would be fine. Good."

"Okay. Good." He was smiling at her again. "What's your name?"

"Lauren."

"Lauren…?"

For a moment she couldn't remember her last name, the one she'd had her whole life. "Kane. Lauren Kane."

"I'm Mike Gibson. Nice to meet you Lauren Kane. Dr. Lauren?" There were little crinkles next to his eyes when he smiled.

"Um, yes. Doctor. Not, you know, M.D. The other kind."

He nodded, that half smile cranked up at her. How did

eyes so dark look that warm?

She totally had to get away from this guy. "Well, bye." She gave him a little wave, then scurried toward her green SUV and didn't glance back at the building until she was safely in her car—with the doors locked and the windows up. Not because she was worried about crime in tiny Tucker, Kentucky, home of the Tuck U Trojans. No, she was worried about protecting herself from the temptation to flirt with Mike Gibson.

He was *not* for her. Nerdy scientist girls had to stay away from hot guys with big, muscle-y arms and white smiles.

So why the heck couldn't she stop looking back at the biology building?

She shook herself. What was wrong with her? She had to get out of here. She could lust after him from a distance. That would be fine. Safe. He could be her pretend lover. She turned the key and threw the car into gear. With one last glance over her shoulder toward her new *imaginary* boyfriend, she stomped her foot on the accelerator.

And promptly shot backward over the curb, knocking over a trash can, which wound up wedged under the rear bumper.

"Gack!" She put the car in park and jumped out to survey the damage. Rounding the back end and seeing the trash can, she shrieked and stepped out of the way of a family of possums—a mom and three…teenagers? They tottered about, blinking in the bright morning sunshine.

"Whoa, careful!" Maintenance Man Mike was suddenly there, grabbing Lauren's upper arms and shifting her out of the way of the scraggly little things. "Are you okay?"

"I'm fine," she said. "But the kids—I ran over their house!" One of the little ones clung to its mother's fur, but two others careened blindly away from the scene of the home wrecking.

"I tell you what," Mike said. "You pull your car forward, off the trash can, then we'll see if we can't help 'em out."

"Okay." Lauren's heartbeat started to slow and beat a regular rhythm. Except where Mike had touched her arms. There, her skin seemed to be throbbing and tingling. *Sheesh.*

She moved her car forward and off of the sidewalk, then went back to Mike and the possums. Fortunately, there were no other faculty members' cars in the lot yet. What would she have told them? *No, I wasn't texting and driving. I was mentally undressing a stranger.*

Oh well. Nothing to do for it but to catch some possums.

The alarm on her phone chimed. She pulled it from her pocket and checked the time. "Shoot."

"Are you late for something?" Mike paused to look at her, pulling on a pair of leather gloves.

"Oh. I'm—I have an eight a.m. class. I was going home to change. But…"

He waved her on. "I got this. I'm a master possum catcher."

"Really?"

"No, but how hard can it be?" He grinned.

Her *parts*—including her brain—tingled. "Are you sure? I can probably—"

"I'm sure," he said. Then that perfect bottom lip curved a little more. "Just watch the road. And try to put the car in drive before you hit the gas this time."

. . .

Mike shook his head as the scientist — *Lauren* — drove away. She was cute in a nerdy, awkward sort of way. Tall, blond, and curvy, but not the type of girl that he usually went for. His brother, Evan — reserved, proper, too-smart Evan — would fit better with her. Hell, Lauren and his brother already worked in the same building. He wondered if Evan had already asked her out, but he wasn't going to ask. He had a goal much more important than pacifying his libido and no business chasing women.

He just needed to keep his head in the game and bring down Dino Romain so he could trade in his Tucker Maintenance ID badge and get back the badge — and gun — that he preferred to carry.

Just thinking about the leader of the Devil's Rangers raised Mike's blood pressure. The fucker had managed to set Mike up as a dirty cop and walk away with a shit-ton of heroin — and now Dino had expanded into the designer drug market. But at least Mike had a line on those drugs. Devil's Dust was being made right here at Tucker University, and Mike was going to find the source, bust Dino, and get his damned job back.

A rustling from beneath the *arbor vitae* lining the walkway reminded him of his current quest. Possum retrieval wasn't part of his plan, either, but he didn't think rescuing animals would cut into his crime fighting time too much. "Come on, Mama," he said.

The mother hissed when he got within three feet of the bush, where she sat squinting at him. Should he call Dylan?

His little brother had a way with animals. One of the only things he was good at, besides getting into trouble. Of course, it was Mike's own fault the kid had slid off the straight and narrow.

Mike had to hope he'd be able to find a way to keep Dylan on track, now that he was at least in school and working.

He checked his watch. Only six thirty? Still too early. Dylan would just get pissed and assume Mike was inventing reasons to check up on him. He gave up on Mama Possum and turned to the nearest baby, which had wandered out from wherever it had been hiding and was making some sort of sound that might be a possum cry. He sighed. He didn't have a chance in a million of keeping his *own* fucked up family together, but maybe he could figure out a way to reunite the over-sized, not-quite-naked mole rats. He crept forward. The baby looked at Mike and keeled over, dead.

Oh, shit! Had he scared it to death? He scooped it up and gave it a cautious poke. It was still breathing.

"Ah. You're playing possum. Funny," he told it before gently lowering it back into the trash can.

"Hey, Mike." Jason Dietz, Mike's maintenance department supervisor, and an old family friend, approached. "What are you doing?"

"Uh, just helping some natural resources along."

"Seriously? You're playing with the possum who lives in the trash can? What's that thing's name on *Sesame Street*? Oliver?" Jason squatted down and made kissy noises. "Come here, Oliver."

"Oscar. Oscar the Grouch. Except this one's a female. She's got babies."

"Come on Oscarina, baby." Jason gave up and straightened. "Anyway, can you go check out the electrical situation in the bio building? The alarms were going off again last night."

"Yeah, someone told me about that. I just finished replacing the card reader on the door. I'll go in a few minutes."

"Your brother thinks there's some sort of disturbance in the Force or something."

"Is the problem in Evan's lab, too?" God forbid his brother's tree frogs be disturbed.

"Nah, it's just in that hot scientist chick's space. You know, the tall blond with the nice, uh..." Jason made the universal sign for bodacious ta-tas.

"If I didn't love you like that inappropriate uncle who shouldn't be invited to Thanksgiving, I might tell you what an asshole you are," Mike said.

Jason shrugged. "But you know exactly who I'm talking about, don't you?"

Mike had a mental vision of the hot scientist—Lauren—with her big amber-colored eyes and a charming blush. And, yeah, maybe a curve of soft breasts pushing against an old Tucker University sweatshirt. Her body was intriguing, but it was Lauren's smile that kicked him in the gut. He shook his head and picked up his tools. "I've got to go get some stuff from the office. I'll head over there after I take care of that plumbing thing in the History department."

"Seriously. You should go for her. She doesn't seem too stuck up to date a man in blue. Even if it's not the kind of blue you want to be wearing. If I wasn't happily married and twice her age..."

Mike laughed in spite of himself. Unfortunately, his real purpose for being here didn't allow for romance. He only had one reason to be on the maintenance crew at Tucker University—and it wasn't to meet women. He had to find where that drug was coming from before it claimed any more victims. He knew that it was being sold to users across the river in Cincinnati by the Devil's Rangers, but if he was going to get his suspension lifted, he had to prove the leader of the gang—Dino Romain—was the link.

Chapter Two

Lauren let herself into the lab after her class, and heard the radio she kept on her desk playing. Weird. She didn't remember turning it on earlier. Especially not to a news station. Probably another issue with her electrical wiring.

"A dangerous new drug is hitting tri-state streets and sending addicts to the emergency room in record numbers. Cincinnati police say they don't know where this drug came from or—"

She snapped it off. Thank God she lived in tiny Tucker, Kentucky—Cincinnati was almost an hour away. It was a college town—hardly immune to recreational drugs, but hopefully the big, bad stuff stayed out of reach in the big city.

She dropped her briefcase next to her desk and booted her ancient laptop, longing for the day when her project was well-funded and she could update her old equipment.

"Hi, Lauren," came a familiar voice from the cell culture room.

Crap. Alex Barker.

She whirled around, frowning. Dealing with the ex-boy-friend-turned-former-coworker was *so* not on her to-do list today. "What are you doing here?"

"I need a flash drive I must have left when I moved out. It's got all my notes from last year on it." He wore a pink, long-sleeved dress shirt, un-tucked, over expensively distressed jeans, and shoes that looked old but probably had been purchased last week at twice Lauren's monthly paycheck.

Huh. He'd aspired to Abercrombie-dom back when he hadn't quite been able to afford it, now it looked like he could. The new University of Cincinnati gig must either be paying pretty well, or he was still living on the edge of his credit limit.

"Oh. I put all that stuff in here." Lauren dug a plastic storage box from under her desk, then handed it to him.

"And I'm popping in for old time's sake." He smiled ruefully, running a hand through his blond hair. Lauren was surprised his fingers didn't get stuck in all the product he used.

"How's the new job?" she asked, though she wasn't sure she wanted to hear about it. The higher paying job at a big-ger university apparently had come with the bonus of an ex-panded ego.

"Good." He started to sort through the miscellaneous junk and didn't look at her when he said, "I could still use a co-investigator. I can see about bringing you on, if you like. You know that if we collaborated, we could do twice as much than we do separately."

"Thanks, but I'm not really interested in starting all

over somewhere new. I'm happy here." Besides, Alex's offer of a good word probably came with the expectation that they would resume their "friend with half-assed benefits" relationship, which had *not* helped her career.

He nodded as though he'd expected her refusal. "I really hope you'll change your mind."

"Alex..."

He crossed his arms and looked at her. "You've got to get over this misplaced fear of losing your seat on the board of directors of Feminists 'R' Us. Working with a man isn't going to wreck your career."

Wow. He'd really never understood her, had he? She counted to ten. Working with a *man* wasn't a problem as long as she wasn't involved—currently or formerly—with him. Working with *Alex* was a problem. He'd tried to take over her projects in the past, which was eerily similar to what had happened to her own mother.

After all, how many times had she heard the story about how her dad had shown up one day and offered to help her mom, a budding scientist, with her project? Nine months later, Karen Kane was a stay-at-home wife and mother— with a useless Ph.D. In addition, only two of Lauren's female friends from grad school had gotten married. The first spent *way* too much time reassuring her husband that she was working in the lab after hours and not cheating. Another had gotten married to another scientist, but then quickly divorced when they couldn't find jobs in the same time zone. Lauren had grown up knowing she wanted to be a scientist, so her option was to give up relationships. She'd tried to have both with Alex, and that hadn't worked. He'd wanted to "help" her—right into obscurity.

She forced a smile. "Thanks anyway, but I think I'll stick around here for a while longer."

Apparently giving up on finding his USB drive, he put the box down next to a pile of lab notebooks. One binder fell off the table with a flutter of pages. "Are you still keeping all of your notes on paper?" he asked, replacing the notebook on the precariously stacked pile. "That's terribly inefficient."

"This is still working pretty nicely." She didn't bother to explain that she'd already started recording her newer data on the computer—he'd probably stay and tell her how to do it right.

Alex wandered over to the complex system of bubbling flasks and tubes that constituted Lauren's research career. "How's the algae growing?" he asked.

She had developed a strain of algae that was going to make her name famous. Actually, the algae *had* her name. *H. kanus.* "It's slow," she said, excitement building the way it did when anyone asked about her algae. "It's growing well enough, but when I process it from step one to step two, I don't get as much product as I was getting a few months ago. At first I thought my student worker had made a mistake, but then I tried it myself and had the same problem. There's something going on during that overnight step, but I'll figure it out."

He nodded, thoughtfully.

Damn. Why'd she go and tell him all that, anyway?

"What about the third step? Is that working?"

"Sure. That seems to be working great. But if I can't get enough of step two to make this commercially viable, the Pemberton Society will never invest in my project. And if I can't get seed money for more preliminary data…"

"You'll never get the NIH past the abstract of your grant." Alex nodded in sympathy. "I heard that the building is having some electrical issues. Maybe that's what's causing the problem with your process."

Lauren shrugged. "Maybe. Evan said he called maintenance to come look at the circuits."

"How *is* Dr. Nerd doing?"

Lauren bristled. "I wish you wouldn't call Evan that."

Thankfully, Alex changed the subject. "What are you going to do if you can't get the Pemberton Group on board?"

"I've applied for every small grant I can think of. Nothing's come through. This is my last chance."

"What about a grant from the Tucker Foundation?"

Lauren laughed. "Miss Emmaline's Kentucky Jelly money?" The elderly woman was well known at Tuck U, having made a success out of her own career as a scientist, studying ways to increase local fruit production. She'd also kept the town of Tucker alive, having provided employment to about half the population—those who didn't work at the college— at her factory.

Alex nodded but frowned. "Why is that so funny? She's got some sort of grant set up for faculty research, doesn't she?"

"Yep. And it comes with conditions that I don't meet."

"What do you mean? I never applied for one of her grants, but I know it's there."

Lauren thought of the eccentric old lady, whom she'd met at a faculty luncheon not too long ago, then explained her reasoning. "The one for this department is for a female scientist who is married."

"Married? Why? I thought Miss Emmie was a feminist

before her time or something."

"I think it's designed to help faculty that are married get jobs at the same institution." Miss Emmie's heart was in the right place, but Lauren only saw marriage as a fast track *out* of research. After all, her own mother was living proof.

A frown marred Alex's forehead, then disappeared. "You know, we could still—"

"Excuse me." A deeply male voice came from the doorway.

Lauren turned to see Mike standing there, in all of his maintenance man manliness. *Dang.* How did he find shirts to fit shoulders that broad? She stepped away from Alex, feeling oddly uncomfortable about talking to her ex-boyfriend… and oddly glad to see the rescuer of possums and all-around perfect male specimen standing in her lab doorway.

• • •

The preppy guy in the pink shirt gave Mike a dirty look, but Mike ignored him. The pretty possum-terrorizing scientist smiled in greeting, and something warm landed in Mike's gut. *Oh, no.* He had a couple of jobs to do—fix shit and find shitty drugs. And he didn't have time to be distracted by Doctor Beautiful.

"Um, hi," she said. "Did you—is the possum family okay?"

"Possum?" asked Pink Shirt, turning to stare at Lauren. "Are you still wasting time with needy wild things?"

Mike looked at the guy, who was now staring at him with a raised eyebrow. The implication was clear. Pink Shirt thought Mike might be one of Lauren's charity cases. What—because he was dressed in a maintenance uniform?

What a douchebag.

Lauren caught his gaze with hers. "It's a long story."

Mike couldn't help himself, he winked.

"Uh-huh." Pinky looked from Lauren to Mike, frowning. This was a guy who didn't like being left out of the joke—if he even had enough of a sense of humor to get it in the first place.

"I'm sorry you couldn't find your flash drive," Lauren said to Pinky. "If I run across it, I'll shoot you an email."

"I can stop by any time," the guy told Lauren. He was clearly reluctant to leave, but he'd been dismissed. Shut down. Kicked to the curb.

Mike stepped up to bat. "I'm here to check your circuits."

It sounded like Pinky said, "I bet you are," as he brushed past on the way through the door.

When Lauren's visitor disappeared, Mike returned to the reason he was there—business. "You say you've got alarms going off for no reason?"

"Yes! Please, come on in," said Lauren.

"Your possums are fine, by the way," he said. "Possum? Possums? I don't know what's right."

She tilted her head, then shrugged. "Oh, who cares? Thanks for taking care of them." She waved her hand in the direction that Pink Shirt had gone. "I have a soft spot for animals."

"Is the guy in the pink shirt one of your critters?" Mike heard himself ask, then mentally slapped himself upside the head. What was he saying? The only fishing he should be doing was to find whoever was making Devil's Dust. "Sorry. None of my business."

Lauren laughed. "No, he was…um, he isn't one of my

critters."

"He wants to be." Damn. More words out of his mouth. He needed to stop that.

"He had his chance." Her clear brown eyes held his for a second before she cleared her throat and said, "So, um, what do you need from me?"

Mike nearly groaned at the thoughts that entered his head—not scratching, biting possums or squealing alarms, but soft touches, sighs, and whispers. He managed to say, "Just going to check your connections. Make sure nothing is sending out too much juice."

"I'll let you get to it," she said then and went to do something to a complex arrangement of glass containers full of bubbling green stuff. Something that involved her bending over to flip a switch on a power strip.

Nice pants. No panty line. Plenty of time on the elliptical trainer.

She straightened and turned.

He thought he pulled his eyes back into his head in time, but wasn't sure. He got his tester out and started checking outlets. "What is all this stuff?" he asked, gesturing to the test tubes. "What kind of research do you do?"

"I could tell you, but then I'd have to kill you," she said.

He laughed. "It looks like pond scum."

"It *is* pond scum." She smiled. "Fancy pond scum. I genetically engineered blue-green algae to produce a morphine analog."

A jolt zinged through Mike that had nothing to do with electricity or sexual attraction. He'd just hit the jackpot.

"Did you say *morphine*?" he asked. "Like, heroin?"

Chapter Three

Wow. Lauren gulped. Her sexy maintenance man was funny and nice and looked at her butt when he thought she wasn't looking. And now he was asking about her research. Her heart *thunked* into her diaphragm, which sent a weird *bloop* into her stomach. And something was happening a little lower, too, but she wasn't going to pay attention to that.

Mike looked at her, clearly waiting for her to say something.

Um, what was the question? Oh, yeah, if her algae made morphine. Duh. "Oh. Sorry. Zoned out for a minute, I'm—getting up too early to deal with all these false alarms has me a little kerfluffled."

He raised his eyebrows and nodded for her to continue.

"So, my algae. Um, so, it's genetically engineered to produce an opioid drug, like heroin or morphine or codeine. Those all come from poppies."

He nodded to show he understood.

"But I put the gene for the drug into the algae DNA. I grow it in these flasks, and then strain it out and dry it down into pellets." She showed him one of the little round chunks of dried algae. "This is called step one. Then there's an extraction step that produces a purified liquid drug. I call that 'step two', because it's, you know, like the second step in the production." God, she sounded dumb. She had an IQ of 161, a perfect score on the ACT, and had made a 2350 on the SAT. But she couldn't talk to this perfectly normal human being without sounding like she'd fallen out of a mall.

"So you make fake heroin. Isn't there already a bunch of stuff like that out there? Like methadone, that kind of thing?"

"Yes. There are several options, and they all have drawbacks. Either they don't work as well or they're also addictive. And unfortunately, step two isn't any improvement over the original drug. I found that if we dry it into a powder and use it that way, it's actually *more* addictive and has a higher mental impairment factor than either morphine or methadone."

He shifted. "How do you know that? Did you try it?"

"Oh! No!" She laughed. "We've given it to mice. They love it. But then they can't remember anything. Like where their food is or who their cage mates are."

"So what the hell are you doing with this stuff?" He seemed tense, as though her answer was going to determine the fate of the free world.

"We process it into step three. It's perfectly safe when it becomes step three. At least for the mice, anyway. It's not addictive, it seems to function perfectly as a pain killer, and it doesn't have any mind- or mood-altering activity."

"Not addictive."

"Yeah," she said. "At step two, it's still addictive and is too much like heroin—gives the same transcendent and euphoric experience along with blocking pain like heroin does *and* has the same highly addictive qualities as heroin, too."

"Huh." Mike leaned back and ran a hand through his thick, dark hair. He stared at her for a moment.

The light feeling in the room had fled.

"It's not going to do anyone any good if I can't figure out why my yield is so much lower now than it used to be, though," she added.

His eyes narrowed. "What do you mean?"

"I'm not getting as much step two as I should when I do the refining step from step one. I set it up to run overnight, and then in the morning I concentrate it and measure it. But there's just never enough."

"Where's it going? Is someone stealing it? It seems like, if it's a drug, it would be attractive to someone wanting a buzz."

She'd wondered about that herself. She remembered the story she'd heard on the radio about a new drug hitting Cincinnati. God, it would be awful if something like that happened with her drug. But there was no way. "No, it's not being stolen. There's always enough extraction liquid in the vial, just not enough product dissolved in the solution. I even tested to make sure someone wasn't taking out the chemical solution and replacing it with water, like mom and dad's liquor. It's all there."

She shrugged. "Anyway, after it's processed, I keep step two locked up. Besides," she added, "I don't think the average person would know what to do with step one. It's pretty gross." She tossed the little chunk she'd showed him into a big black zipper bag full of pellets and held it out for him to see. "It looks like rabbit food, but smells like something you'd feed fish."

He leaned over and sniffed, then drew back, nose wrinkled. "So, the drug is in there?"

"Yeah. When we first transfected the gene into the algae, we fed the pellets to the mice. They weren't too crazy about it. We thought about vaporizing it…you know, like medical marijuana, or something, but that was before we realized how addictive it is in its native form."

"So you could smoke it?"

She paused and stared at him, wondering why he was so interested.

He shrugged. "I watch a lot of *CSI*."

"Oh, me, too! I love *CSI*." And *Law and Order*. And *Bones*. And *NCIS*. But he didn't need to know every show she watched. "I guess you *could* smoke the algae, though I think it wouldn't taste very good." Not to mention the fact that the binding agents she'd added would be poisonous and could cause brain damage.

"Drug users don't really care about that."

Drug users didn't care about much except scoring drugs, at least according to the news. And *CSI* and *Law and Order* and *Bones* and *NCIS*. She narrowed her eyes and examined Mike. He was dangerous-looking, though she thought he looked too fit and clear-eyed to be a drug user himself.

"How do you get the drug out of the dried junk?"

There was another bag of pellets on the counter, and he started to reach for it at the same time she did. Her hand covered his before she could change direction. The heat of his hand, big and rough-knuckled, beneath hers, seared her palm.

Their eyes met for a split second before she casually extracted the bag from his hand. At least, she hoped she looked casual. That touch had turned her more upside down than she'd want to admit. She put the bag into a plastic bin marked with the day's date. She'd have to remember to take it with her when she left. Nodding to a bench stocked with centrifuge tubes and bottles of buffers, she said, "I use a bunch of chemicals to extract the compound, some others to alter the structure, then concentrate it." She stopped, wondering if she'd gone into too much detail. At least she hadn't started naming molecular formulas. But the way Mike stared, he seemed to still be interested. She pointed at the little safe. "Then I stash it in the safe until I test it."

"Are you the only worker here? Or do you have an assistant, or whatever?"

What was with all the questions? Was he uber nosey, bored with work, or flirting? Probably not the third option, although she wasn't sure she'd even know what flirting looked like, it had been so long. As in, so long that the last hot guy who flirted with her was…imaginary. "If I can get the grant I'm hoping for, I'll have enough to support a graduate student and a technician. I have a student worker in the meantime. Dylan White. He's great…ten hours a week, and he does the work of a full time technician."

"Wait—Dylan works for *you*?" Mike's jaw tightened and his brows lowered, eyes narrowing.

"Do you know him?"

"He's my little brother."

His *brother*? Why was he so…unhappy? Dylan was the

sweetest kid—and the best student worker she'd ever had. Okay, so he was the first one she'd had to herself, but as a grad student and post-doc, she'd supervised quite a few useless occupiers of lab coats. Dylan wasn't one of the slackers, and she was going to defend him. "No kidding? That's so cool! Dylan's awesome. I really like having him here."

Mike didn't seem to know what to say to that. "Oh. That's...great. I guess."

Then something struck Lauren. "So if Dylan's your brother, and Evan Adams is Dylan's brother, that makes you—"

Mike sighed. "Also Evan's brother."

"But you told me your last name is Gibson."

"Yep. We have three different dads. Had. Different dads."

Well, Lauren had certainly stepped in something here. She hadn't pried into Dylan's family history, other than knowing that his brother was the professor across the hall. They seemed to get along okay, although it would be a challenge for anyone to be close to Evan. He was so...uptight.

"So you all grew up here in Tucker," she said.

"More or less."

She was treading close to *The Land of Getting To Know You*, and warning bells chimed in the distance, but the *Here's A Guy Who Listens To You Without Telling You What To Do* monitor shushed them. "Did you work for Kentucky Jelly, too?" Tucker was home to the Kentucky Jelly plant, the only other business in town besides the University.

"Miss Emmaline was one of my grandmother's best friends, and she put me to work as soon as it was legal for me to get a paycheck. I think that if you didn't put in your time in the bottling plant, you didn't get a high school diploma."

"That's awesome. I grew up in Columbus. Not exactly The Big Apple, but too big to know everyone, unlike here."

"Is your family still close by?" Mike asked.

Oh, goody. And here he came, meeting her in the demilitarized *Zone of Small Talk*. "Close enough. My dad's on the faculty at Ohio State. I think maybe I should have gone a little farther than two and a half hours away," she said.

"I have a feeling that family finds us no matter how far we try to go."

Lauren laughed, liking this flirting thing in spite of herself. This *was* flirting, right? *Ye gads*. How was she supposed to know?

"So is your dad a scientist, too?"

It must be flirting, because why else would he be asking all this mundane get-to-know-you stuff?

"Yep."

"That's cool. You followed in his footsteps, huh?"

"Well, more like picked up where my mom left off. She was a scientist, too, before she had me."

"And raising a baby human took the place of raising lab rats?"

"Something like that." Well, not exactly, but it wasn't like she was going to share the story of her mom losing her career to motherhood with Mike The Hot Maintenance Guy. At least her mom had made her childhood fun. She smiled, thinking of the white mice she'd been allowed to keep when she was a kid. Watson and Crick.

He smiled back at her. His eyes held hers for just a moment longer than was strictly necessary. She realized she was standing a little closer to him than strictly necessary, too, and that she had a strand of hair twisted around her index finger.

She unwound it and tucked it behind her ear.

He cleared his throat and stepped back. "Listen, I think your electrical circuits are fine. There's got to be something a little deeper in the system going on here. I'll get Jason to call the electrician the university has under contract."

"Okay. Well, thanks for stopping in. And for, you know, chasing Alex off."

"Thanks for telling me about your project. You must be a good teacher, because even a grunt like me understood most of that." He picked up his toolbox. "We'll figure out where your step two product is going, one way or another."

Something about the way he said that gave her pause. Since when had Tucker University started hiring maintenance men who doubled as research consultants?

• • •

Of course, Mike ran into Evan when he left Lauren's lab. Almost literally.

"Watch where you're going, Michael!" Evan said, stepping aside. He smoothed an imaginary stray hair back in place.

Mike took a deep breath and let it out slowly, refraining from biting the head off his anal-retentive brother. He was still reeling from the knowledge that he'd been stumbling around Tucker University for a week trying to find out where the hell Devil's Dust was coming from and his own punky little brother was working with it every day. In fact, both of his brothers were in spitting distance of the drug. Although Evan couldn't have been considered punky since... ever. He *could* be considered someone Mike had no desire to talk to right now, however.

He wanted time to let his mind chew on the information he'd just taken in and digest it into something that made sense. How was it that the adorable scientist Lauren Kane was the one making the formula for Devil's Dust? And more importantly, how was it that the drug was getting off the campus and onto the streets?

"Where's the inferno?" Evan asked, then when Mike glared at him, he amended that to, "Is something wrong?"

"Did you know Dylan was working in a lab where dangerous drugs are being made?"

Evan's lips tightened. "Yes. And I've spoken with him about it. He assured me that he's keeping his nose clean, and I believe him."

"Really?" Mike wondered if it was his own suspicious—okay, paranoid—nature that made Evan seem so naive.

"Really."

"Does he have keys to everything? Can he come and go at all hours?"

Evan blinked. "He can get into the building any time with his student ID, but he'd have to have a key to the lab. I think he only works when Lauren's working."

"I don't like this."

Evan opened his mouth, then closed it again, like he wanted to say something more.

"What?"

"Are you really in a position to judge?"

Part of him—the proud, defensive part—wanted to make Evan understand that he wasn't the fuck up that everyone believed him to be, but he didn't see any point.

Ironic. He could only *ask* someone to believe that he

hadn't been responsible for the fuck up that had cost him his job—and nearly gotten Dylan killed. Until he could prove who was making and distributing Devil's Dust and bring them to justice, that is. And right there, smack dab in the middle of his brothers, was a lab making some kind of heroin alternative. His gut said Lauren was innocent, but his instincts had failed him in the past.

He needed to find out more about Lauren Kane.

Maybe Evan knew something that would help. He seemed to have an opinion about Dylan's work situation.

"I was wondering—"

"Chief Crawford asked about you," Evan said.

"Did he?" Great. "How is Dwayne?"

"Disappointed that you haven't contacted him since you moved back to Tucker," Evan said.

"I'm not sure—'"

"I know that you think he's disappointed in you because of your troubles, but I believe he's a fairly forgiving person," Evan told him.

Mike snorted. Crawford had better be *forgiving*, after all of the shit Dwayne had done in high school that Mike could use as blackmail material, were he so inclined. But he hadn't contacted his old friend because he didn't want to hear Crawford tell him he was tilting at windmills in his quest to find the source of Devil's Dust.

"As a matter of fact," Evan continued, "he said he was disappointed that you didn't come to him when you moved back to town. Apparently, the Tucker Police Department has an opening."

"I'm still technically employed by another department," Mike said.

It was Evan's turn to snort. "'Suspended indefinitely, without pay', sounds a lot like fired to me. I don't know why you'd want to go back there, even if you were able to prove your innocence. And if you could work for someone who trusts you, like Crawford…"

Mike just shook his head. He wasn't going to get into his desire for justice and redemption. "I'll give Dwayne a call." One of these days.

"Don't forget dinner this weekend," Evan said. "You agreed to bring the starchy side dish."

"Potatoes. Yeah. I remember."

"Or pasta, or rice. It doesn't have to be—"

"Dylan wants Grandma's cheesy potatoes." Enough of the dinner discussion. He needed info on how Devil's Dust was leaving campus, not a menu.

"Okay, potatoes," Evan said. "And yourself. No matter how much you might want to drop off food and run, Grandma wanted us to have a home cooked meal *together*. We all promised her."

"Grandma was out of her sweet mind with dementia when we made that promise," Mike said. "She thought we were Great Uncle Samuel and Mom."

Evan raised his eyebrows.

Mike pinched the bridge of his nose. "Okay. I'll be there. Sunday. Five thirty."

Evan nodded.

"I wonder if you—"

"There you are, Evan!" An old guy came around the corner, wearing a lab coat that fell all the way to the tops of his shiny saddle shoes.

Evan shot Mike an apologetic look. "This will take a while," he muttered, then turned to Mr. Frump. "Hello, Dr. Jerrold."

"I'll talk to you later," Mike said, putting aside finding out how Lauren Kane's drug—if it was her drug—was getting out of her lab and into the noses and veins of drug addicts.

"Have a good afternoon," Evan said, and with that, he stepped around his brother and proceeded down the hall.

Mike tilted his head until his neck cracked, and then repeated the move on the other side. It was no use. He was going to have to hit the Advil. And he needed to connect with Dylan to ask him what he knew about Lauren's algae and Devil's Dust. At least he finally had a lead. Even if it was his own kid brother.

• • •

After a long day of responding to calls about keys that didn't fit in locks, overflowing dorm toilets, and windows that wouldn't open, Mike tossed his tool belt behind the seat of his old F-150 and climbed into the cab. He'd rather have been back working as a cop—even directing traffic if he couldn't be a detective again. But this maintenance gig was coming in pretty handy right now.

When he'd been fired, he'd already had a lead on where the Devil's Dust was coming from—the university. He just needed a good excuse to be on campus. Pretending to be a student wouldn't have worked—he'd have stood out like a sore thumb. So he'd called Jason, the maintenance supervisor, who had worked for Evan's dad, Lloyd, back in the day. Lloyd taught Mike everything he knew about fixing stuff and had been more of a dad than Mike's own sperm donor. Jason hired Mike, no questions asked.

The day had been long and relatively boring, but at least he'd found out where Devil's Dust was most likely being created. What he hadn't been able to do was get ahold of Dylan, no matter that he'd tried every which way to Sunday to find him today. Damned kid. The delinquent knew it made Mike bat-shit crazy when he couldn't find him.

He stuck his key in the ignition and prayed the old truck would start. It growled to life, and after coughing a few times, settled into a steady rumble. Too bad Dylan's mechanic dad had been too busy shooting up heroin and beating his step-sons to show them how to do a tune-up on a vehicle.

As the truck warmed up, he stared through the bug-splattered windshield at the biology building, simultaneous-ly hoping for a sight of the sexy scientist and chiding himself for it. Then, as though Mike had mentally summoned her, Lauren came through the building's front door, carrying a plastic grocery bag. She skipped down the steps and looked toward the parking lot, right where Mike was parked. The moment she locked gazes with him, she hesitated and lost her footing, flailing awkwardly for a moment. Mike grabbed the door handle, planning to scoop her up if she fell, but she regained her balance. A black plastic bag, like the one she'd shown him a few hours ago, had fallen out of the plas-tic grocery bag and landed on the bottom step. After quickly glancing around, she picked it up, wrapped the remnants of the grocery bag around it, and tucked it under her arm. She stepped up her pace and hurried toward her car.

What the hell? Was she taking the drug with her? So much for being sure she was innocent. Looked like he'd be taking a little drive before going home tonight. The cute sci-entist needed a little following.

Chapter Four

In the parking lot of the Tucker Animal Welfare Society where she volunteered, Lauren squinted against the late afternoon sunlight as she handed a bag of fortified rat pellets to her elderly friend, Rick. When he'd called her earlier in the day and mentioned he was about out of food, she'd agreed to meet him here with a load of yummies for Nibbles. It bugged her to no end that she had to *steal* trash so that the aging guy's aging rat could eat well. The animals in the biology building lived better than most humans, and their chow was top of the line. When new shipments of food were brought in, the almost-empty bags were tossed out, meaning loads of perfectly good food was thrown away. So every now and then, Lauren scooped up a bag and brought it to the shelter for Rick's rat. On a strict budget, the senior had enough trouble buying healthy food for himself, never mind his pet.

Yeah, it was just a rat, and yeah, rats could survive on

almost anything, but Nibbles was special to the old guy, and Lauren was a soft touch.

The old man thanked her for her trouble and got into his car.

It was really no trouble, since she had to come out here to medicate Miss Posey, the decrepit cat who was probably yowling away inside the cinder-brick sanctuary. And coming out here to feed Miss Posey had been a good excuse to send Alex's last phone call to voicemail.

She felt kind of bad about that, but she'd just seen him and hadn't been in the mood to be friendly. And sure enough, his message was an offer to stop by and show her how he thought she should scan all of her hand written notes into digital form with an app he'd found on one of his email loops. Even though she could use the help, he was just try-ing to find an excuse to spend time with her, and she needed to cut that cord. They had been coworkers for so long—she never should have stepped over the line with him and gotten intimate.

Rick tooted the horn and turned to wave at her, then pulled out of the parking lot, right into the path of a big pickup truck that was pulling in. *Crap*. She hated turning away prospective owners, but it wasn't an adoption night. The shelter was closed. Who was this?

The truck's movement changed the angle of the sunlight that had been reflecting off of the windshield, and Lauren saw the driver.

What the heck? Was that Mike Gibson?

He noticed her at the same time she saw him, and even though she gave him a friendly grin, the look he put on his face was priceless—if one tried to put value on expressions of dismay.

Well, she hadn't expected to see him, either. Besides, she already knew she needed to stay away from him, so the fact that he didn't appear thrilled to see her should have been a good thing. Except her feelings had taken a little nosedive when he didn't smile back. She seriously needed to get a grip.

• • •

Shit! The truck resisted when Mike yanked the steering wheel. He managed to miss the dusty Honda by a hair and land the F-150 inches from the edge of a drainage ditch. The truck stalled, however, as the other car putted away. He cranked the starter, but he'd nicknamed the beast Old Faithful out of irony, not because the name fit. *Damn it.* He turned to watch the vehicle gain momentum as it headed down the road. There went the package of algae pellets, he'd bet his tool belt on it.

"Are you okay?" Lauren appeared, her hand on his window frame, peering in at him.

"Yeah," he muttered.

"Well, then, hi, Mike!"

"Hi, Lauren," he said, after a beat. "What are you doing here?" What else was he gonna say? *Hi, where is that bag of dried drug stuff you showed me earlier today?*

"Um…I volunteer here a couple of times a week. What brings *you* out this way tonight?" She rambled a little, as though she were nervous. Because she was doing something wrong? Or was it him who made her nervous? "Are you interested in adopting a pet? We're closed, but I've got to do something inside anyway, if you'd like to come in and look around."

He glanced at the building behind her. Huh. It was an animal shelter. "Um…" He scratched his chin, a day's worth of stubble rasping under his fingers. He'd lost the guy in the Honda, who might—or might not—have the drugs in his car, but he might as well find out what Lauren was up to here. He scrambled to come up with an answer. "I…uh…yeah. I was thinking about looking into getting a dog—something Dylan could take care of, learn some responsibility, but if you're closed, I don't want to put you to any trouble."

"It's no trouble! Let's see who we have that might suit you." Her sunny smile was so guileless that Mike was strangely ashamed that he was only pretending to want a dog. He opened his mouth, then shut it again, and opened the truck door. He looked toward the road one more time, then turned back to her, smiled, and said, "Fine. Let's take a look."

Lauren unlocked the big metal door and headed inside. He followed her in, only to be greeted by a cacophony of meows, woofs, and an occasional…bray? It took him a moment to readjust to the sudden wave of sound, and he looked around for Lauren. Aaaand there she was, bending over in those pants again to lift a cat into her arms.

He looked away—he should be mentally measuring the building for clandestine drug manufacturing space. "Does this building have a basement?"

"Huh?"

Subtle, Sherlock. He thought fast. Difficult when his brain was vacationing in his pants. "On the way over here, I was listening to a news story about tornados."

She seemed to accept this, started to speak, but he cut her off.

"I guess a cinder block building doesn't need a storm cellar. Just a big internal storage room or something." *Yes*, he was still the master of redirection.

"Well, we don't have one of those, either, but then we aren't in Kansas, right? Or a trailer park *anywhere*."

"Good point."

"What made you decide to adopt a pet *today*?" she asked, emphasis on today.

He needed a dog like he needed—well, he didn't need a dog. Or a cat. Or a bird. Not even a fish, for that matter. "I heard this place was here, and I wasn't doing anything else, so—"

Her face lit up. "You've heard of us? That's so cool. We're kind of new, so it's great to know that the community's taking notice." She put the gray tiger cat on the floor, and it sauntered to a chair and jumped onto the seat.

"As a volunteer, what do you do here?" he asked. He wondered what she would say. He guessed "making drug deals" wasn't going to be her answer.

She went to a cabinet behind the counter of the little office and took out a prescription bottle. "I'm the drug pusher," she said.

The look on his face must have given away his thoughts, because she grinned.

"Kidding! We have an old cat who's just getting over pneumonia, and she needs antibiotics. And an antidepressant, because she's…well, anyway, you'll meet her soon enough. The day person, Carol, dosed Posy before she left at lunch time, but I promised I'd take the night shift."

"So you work here nights, even after you're done doing mysterious science stuff?"

She laughed, a pure, sweet sound, and something zinged through him.

"I'm never done doing science stuff," she admitted, "although, I sneak away now and then. But this isn't work." She picked up a package of cat treats and gestured toward another door. "We'll just go through here."

The room they entered had a wall of cages housing a variety of sleeping, meowing, and hissing cats—and one rabbit. The bottommost cage on the right side was draped with a towel. Lauren knelt down next to it and said, "Miss Posy, time for your medicine."

When the most horrendous growl Mike had ever heard from a living creature came from behind the towel, Lauren looked up at him and shrugged. He tried not to notice that her top pulled down and displayed *almost* enough cleavage. *Completely* enough would be if that top accidentally shredded and floated away.

Aaaaand she was on her knees in front of him. He cleared his throat and squatted next to her.

"She's a little grumpy by nature," Lauren told him. "Actually…it might be good that you stopped by. She doesn't like most people, but she seems to hate men less. Maybe you can hold her while I give her the pill."

"Why is she behind a towel? Is she shy or something?" Or was the cat hiding a brick of illegal drugs?

"Or something. She just seems to like being in the dark." Lauren pulled the towel aside, and Mike came face-to-face with the biggest, ugliest orange cat he'd ever seen. But no Devil's Dust, unless the beast was responsible for creating it from the bowels of hell. Its eyes didn't quite glow with demon fire, but...

"Holy shit," he said.

The cat hissed.

"Now, Miss Posy, come on. It's time for your goody." Lauren turned away to open the pill container, taking one out and wrapping it in a piece of something soft and squishy. She looked at Mike. "If she sees me open the container, she won't come out at all."

She turned back around and showed the glob to the cat. "Lookie here! Treats!"

Mike was charmed in spite of himself.

"Okay, I'll open the cage, you reach in and grab her."

"Are you sure she won't scratch my eyes out?"

Lauren smiled at him. "Nope. But you're the Possum Wrangler, right? You're probably braver than the Crocodile Hunter. I'm pretty sure you can take on one little old lady."

"Elderly human ladies are my specialty." Mike thought about his grandma and how he'd always managed to convince her to slip him an extra cookie after dinner, and her old friend Miss Emmie, who seemed to have a soft spot for him. "Not so sure about old cats."

But he reached into the cage anyway and took out the giant cat. Its hair was matted in some places and missing in others. He held her around the middle, legs splayed, facing Lauren, who shook her head. Guess she was serious about him holding the cat. He tucked the beast against his chest. The damned thing started growling again.

"She likes you!"

"She's growling at me."

"That's purring." Lauren expertly pried the cat's mouth

open and shoved in the pill. Her head was inches from his face, and he breathed in lemons and flowers.

Mike cautiously shoved the thing back into its cage, where it turned and glared at him.

Lauren shook her head. "I don't know if she's going to make it much longer." She looked like she might cry.

"Why? You're giving her medicine."

"Yes, but she's got a nervous condition, which seems to be made worse by being here at the shelter. She doesn't get along with the other animals. She scratches at herself constantly and keeps getting abscesses. If we can't get her adopted, I'm afraid we'll have to have her put to sleep."

"Why don't you take her home?" he asked. Lauren seemed like the type who would take in ugly strays on a regular basis. Hell, she was being nice to him.

"Kevin doesn't like her."

"You're married?" *Aw, hell.* He hadn't meant to ask that. He didn't care if she was involved with someone or not. Well, maybe he did. But not because he was interested in her. If she was involved with someone, he needed to know if they were part of whatever was going on with the disappearance of the drugs from her lab.

She laughed. "Kevin's my cat. I took Miss Posy home overnight once, and it got bloody. No, I'm single. Um…" She shook her head, and Mike detected a faint blush. "Do you want to see the dogs? We've got an awesome lab mix. He's perfect for a guy. He loves to play catch."

Playing catch sounded do-able.

However, fifteen minutes later, he was the shell-shocked foster dad of a cat. Not an energetic, mixed-breed dog who would play catch and be a girl-magnet, but one very ugly, very neurotic cat. Lauren had convinced him that, even though the damned thing needed medicine twice a day, it would be lower maintenance than a dog, and fit into his and Dylan's irregularly scheduled lifestyles better. The way she looked at him, like he was some kind of a hero, made it almost worthwhile. He was only keeping it until they found another home for it, though.

"Your name's not staying Miss Posy," he told the thing as it dug its claws into the upholstery of his truck. It glared and snarled. He slammed the door, which bounced open again. He grabbed the cat before she made a break for it and repeated the process. On the third try, the door stayed shut. He turned to find Lauren had followed him out of the building.

"What are you going to call her?" she asked.

"Possum."

She grinned, but then her expression grew into a hot stare that traveled from his eyes to the vicinity of his mouth. His own gaze moved along a similar path over her face, but he didn't stop at her mouth. He went as far as to see the blush that stained her upper chest and the slight rise of hard nipples behind bra and sweater.

Okay, he admitted it. He wanted her. Shit, he'd just named his fucking cat after the very moment they'd met, a whopping twelve hours ago.

Her chest rose and fell. He looked back at her face, and he realized that *she* realized he'd been staring at her breasts. And was smiling shyly instead of looking offended. He needed to get out of there before he kissed her. Hell, he already needed to adjust his jeans.

He stepped away and shoved a hand through his hair. He hadn't found anything fishy at the shelter, in spite of asking every question he could think of to get her to show him the facility. There was no mysterious room full of Bunsen burners and barrels of chemicals or anything, no boxes filled with empty drug vials, waiting to be filled.

He couldn't think of another reason to stick around. Not one that didn't involve pressing Lauren up against the side of his truck and kissing the hell out of her. "I guess I'll see you later."

She nodded, then licked her lips and said, "Um, yeah. Okay. If you—" She gestured to the newly christened and howling Possum. "If you need any help, advice or anything, let me know."

He waited while she started her car before he started his truck and pulled onto the road.

Shit.

He didn't know any more about the Devil's Dust situation than he had when he got here. He'd thought the drug was probably being cooked in some basement somewhere, but after hearing about Lauren's research, he wasn't so sure. But there was no way she was a drug dealer—neurotic cats aside—was there? But what about that bag of pellets she'd carried out of the building earlier? He was going to have to manage to spend more time with her to find out what she was up to.

Chapter Five

Possum The Cranky Cat spent the ride from the shelter tucked beneath Mike's legs, which made lifting his foot from gas to brake pedal a painstaking operation — but they made it to the local Food Giant without too much arguing. Until he came out of the store, that is, arms laden with litter box, litter, food, and toys — and found the upholstery shredded.

"I was only gone for ten minutes!" he told the cat when he opened the door. She hissed at him, then jumped into the passenger seat and started licking her paw. "Seriously? The seats are the only part of this truck that aren't messed up. At least they *were*."

He climbed in and started the engine, waving at old Miss Emmaline Tucker as she crept across the parking lot. The woman's frail appearance belied her powerful position in the community as the brains behind Kentucky Jelly and the Tucker Foundation. He sighed when she waved at him to open his window. How she could see him, as bent over as she was, was beyond him. She'd been one of his grandmother's best friends, so he couldn't pretend he didn't see her.

"Hi, Miss Emmie."

"Hi yourself. I see you've moved back to town."

"Yes ma'am."

"That's good. Your grandma would be happy to see that you're in her old house instead of selling it. Happier if you'd done it before she went to her great reward, but still. She's probably up there smiling on you now."

Mike doubted that, given the mess he'd made of his life so far, but he nodded and said, "Thank you. I like to think so."

"Do you like working with my son-in-law?"

Mike's boss Jason was married to Miss Emmie's daughter Louella. Jason referred to himself and his bride as the divine debutante and the dumbass, but they seemed to be as much in love now as any two people could be.

"Jason's a good guy," Mike said.

"Of course he is. And how are you doing with Dylan?"

Leave it to Miss Emmie to cut to the chase. "We're holding it together," he lied.

She glared at him. "Bullshit. I bet you fight like cats and dogs." She shook her head. "I know you promised your grandma before she died that you'd look after him, and you're probably doing a better job than you think, especially after that little fuck up in Cincinnati."

Mike barked out a laugh at the language that came out of the prim little old lady. "Which fuck up are you referring to? Mine or his?"

"Watch your language," she snapped, but then smacked him on the shoulder with a gnarled hand and gave him a sly smile. "You met any hot chicks since you moved back to town?"

He thought of Lauren, but said only, "No, ma'am, I'm staying out of the dating business. I don't seem to be much good at choosing nice girls. Unless you're available?"

She snorted but smiled anyway, then patted him on the arm and said, "You take care, now. And don't be afraid to step out and meet somebody. I hear that there's a pretty lady scientist over on the campus who might be single. Not too many girls as smart as me in the department these days."

How did she know Lauren? Miss Emmaline had probably run across her at some sort of fancy University event. Emmie was a huge donor to the various charities on campus. "Well, if I change my mind, I'll certainly ask for an introduction."

"Ha. Unlikely. You aren't known for your willingness to ask for help." Her eyes narrowed. "I know people who could have fixed that mess you got yourself into a few months ago."

What Mike knew was that if he'd called Miss Emmie for help, she would have pulled strings and covered up the whole thing, and he also knew that secrets like that required bribes and almost never remained buried. No way was he going to try to make two wrongs into a right.

Mike said goodbye and tried again to call Dylan. Either his brother was ignoring him, or he had lost his phone again. He really needed to find out what Dylan knew about Lauren's missing drug, and if there was any way that it could be Devil's Dust. Given his past history with the Devil's Rangers, it seemed more and more likely that the kid was up to his neck in trouble — again.

The house was quiet when he got home, and he left the cat in the truck for a few minutes while he took his supplies inside. He looked at the corner of the laundry room where

Dylan's skateboard rested next to a baseball bat and glove that were dustier than Grandma's Hummel collection. He thought about pitching them but was a little nostalgic for the days when they'd stayed with Grandma when they were younger, and he and Evan had played catch with the much younger Dylan—though he'd have his fingernails pulled out with hot tweezers before he let anyone know what a sap he was. Instead, he shoved the stuff in the hall closet and made a kitty latrine.

By the time he got the litter box set up and convinced Possum to leave her new favorite scratching post—his truck—it was fully dark.

"Come on," he told her while she transferred her claws to his shirt. "You know, if I have to get clawed, I'd rather it be by my own species." Lauren's elegant fingers came to mind, and then her long, trim body. He thought about her digging her nails into him as he went into her. The cat growled and fought to escape his hold, breaking his fantasy. Just as well. He had some internet research to do before turning in for the night, and he needed to get his mind back into the head on his shoulders.

Behind him, he heard the familiar screech of brakes on Dylan's bike. Mike turned, and for once, Dylan's face wasn't folded into a sneer or, worse, flatly expressionless.

After dismounting, Dylan hitched his backpack higher on his shoulders and stared at the near-bald yowling ball of nasty in Mike's arms. "What's that?"

"I adopted a cat. Or signed up to be a foster person."

"That's cool."

As his brother got closer, Mike was assaulted with an overwhelming wave of— "Dude, did you get a new cologne?"

"Yeah. You like it?"

For an instant, the cool bravado that Dylan wore like armor slipped, and Mike masked his reaction to the god-awful scent. "Um—"

Possum yowled. *Saved by the cat.*

Dylan reached a hand toward Possum, who hissed and took a swipe at him. He jerked back and laughed, a sound nearly foreign to Mike's ears. "Okay. I'll let you get settled. What's his name?"

Seeing the smile on the kid's face made Mike doubt his suspicion that Dylan was in trouble.

"*Her* name is Possum." At Dylan's raised eyebrows, Mike said, "Long story." Dylan followed him up the sidewalk and into the house.

"What did you do with my shit?" Dylan asked, scowling at the space currently filled with a litter box.

Of course he'd immediately focus on how this cat would inconvenience him, even though the stuff Mike had moved hadn't been used in years, as far as he could tell. "It's safe, don't panic. I put it in the closet."

"I wasn't panicking, I just asked a question. Christ."

"Don't swear. And don't be so defensive." Mike realized as soon as it came out of his mouth that he shouldn't have said that last part.

"Okay, *Mom*," Dylan said. "I just asked a question. You're so worried about everything I say and how I say it."

"You don't want to go there," Mike said. Less than two minutes together and they were already at each other's throats. He might not trust his brother, but he'd promised their grandmother—on her deathbed—that he'd look out for his siblings. Evan hadn't needed Mike in a long time, but

Dylan had, and Mike had failed him—miserably. He sighed. "Look. I didn't mean anything by that."

"Whatever." Dylan opened the refrigerator, and then closed it again. "We need groceries."

"We always need groceries."

"Why didn't you get food when you picked up the cat supplies?"

"I didn't want to leave her alone in the car for too long. Do you want to order a pizza?"

Dylan walked to the freezer and opened it, displaying a half dozen frozen pizzas.

"I bet Evan's got roast beef and fresh organic green beans tonight, or eggplant parmesan and tofu muffins. You could call him." Mike tried to keep the defensive tone out of his own voice.

A reluctant smile crossed Dylan's face. "Yeah, but then I'd have to listen to a lecture on the decay of modern society as a result of poor hygiene and video game-induced ADHD."

"True that. See how lucky you are to be stuck with me?"

Dylan shook his head. "As long as I can keep ignoring you, and you keep ignoring me, we'll probably be okay."

Mike started to speak, then thought better of it and said instead, "Speaking of ignoring you, where were you tonight?"

Taking a gallon of milk from the fridge, Dylan removed the lid and sniffed. He shrugged, then turned to get a glass. He poured his drink, then lied straight to Mike's face. "I was helping my boss, Dr. Kane, at her lab."

His boss, Dr. Kane, who had been with Mike at the animal shelter. How fucking dumb did Dylan think he was? And whose ass was he trying to cover—his own, or someone else's?

Chapter Six

Why did mornings have to be so damned bright? Couldn't one just ease into the day with gradually increasing light? Oh yeah. One could. If one got up *before* the sun. But Lauren had experienced her dawn's early light for the year yesterday.

She slammed the door of her aging Ford Explorer and heard something crunch inside the panel. She looked, but didn't see any stray car bits laying around the parking space. Hopefully, whatever it was wouldn't wind up costing too much to fix. If she were really lucky, it would be a random gremlin noise and not even be anything that *needed* fixing. Until proven otherwise, she was going with that hypothesis. She was pretty good at ignoring problems unless they interrupted her workflow. Hoisting her bag over her shoulder, she walked toward the Bio building.

The trash can serving as a possum home rattled, and she dropped in a handful of dry cat food as she passed.

Lauren pulled open the door to the building, annoyed with herself for looking to see if Mike was anywhere nearby. She paused, taking a moment to appreciate the ancient part of the building, and breathed deep, the scents of old wood, a little mildew, strong coffee, and the faintest undertone of sweat socks filling her lungs. The coffee scent was pleasant—the sweat socks, not so much—but it was all part of her home turf, and she loved it.

She mounted the worn marble steps to the second floor and pushed through a set of double fire doors to the new wing, where her lab sat behind a steel door, in sterile brightness, between other clean, shiny labs.

She needed to focus on her presentation to the Pemberton people—the one where she explained about her study and begged for funding—but after her interesting run-in with Mike The Hot Maintenance Man the night before, funding wasn't front and center in her mind—Mike was. Something told her he hadn't stopped by intending to adopt a pet. Had he gone there because he was interested in her? Maybe? She was pretty sure she'd caught him checking out her boobs. And he'd gotten that look on his face that sometimes meant a guy was about to kiss her. Except the usual guy who wanted to kiss *her* wasn't generally someone she wanted to kiss back—so she could be very wrong about that body language. There was certainly nothing *usual* about Mike Gibson.

If he wanted to see her, why go all the way out to the shelter? Why not just visit her again at work? Maybe he had some sort of thing against flirting on company time. But then, if he was interested in her, why didn't he ask her out? Not that she was going to go out with him, anyway, but she wanted to know what was going on. She was a scientist. That's what scientists did. They solved interesting puzzles—they didn't moon around, obsessing over hot maintenance men.

As she rounded the corner at the end of the hall, she saw what appeared to be all of her co-workers standing in the hall outside of her lab. When someone saw her, a murmur went through the crowd, and everyone—like some sort of a departmental cyborg—turned to look at her.

"What's going on?" Was there a dead custodian in her lab? That had happened to someone she'd known in grad school. A professor came in one morning and found one of the cleaning staff dead on the floor of his lab. Apparently, the guy had a bit of a drinking problem and had decided to sample the alcohols that were stored in the flammable cabinet. Unfortunately, the custodian hadn't understood that "methanol" wasn't interchangeable with the drinkable "ethanol" and had poisoned himself. It was a messy way to die.

The group outside of her door parted and Dr. Hector Jerrold, the department chair, stepped forward, running a gnarled hand through his thick, gray hair. He looked like an overweight, Hispanic Einstein. Wait—Jerrold was there? A sudden jolt of adrenaline hit her. *Uh oh*. It must be bad if the old man left his hallowed office. This was not going to be good.

"Lauren," he began, then stopped and looked back through the door of her lab. He didn't smile.

She forced her lungs to push air over her vocal cords, her lips to move. "Is everything okay?"

Hector frowned. "I don't know how to tell you this—"

By this time, Lauren was almost even with the door, so

she took a few more steps forward and looked inside. After her heart started sending blood back through her brain, she recognized utter destruction.

There were broken bottles and beakers on every surface, liquid dripping from the blue composite counters. Books and papers were scattered, pages torn out and soaked. Her little centrifuge was tipped over, the electronics ripped out of it. The scale was crushed.

"Lauren, I don't know what to say."

She took a deep breath and her brain kicked back into gear. "Oh, God. My algae."

• • •

"Hey, bud. Perfect timing."

"S'up?" Mike barely glanced at Jason as he walked into the office and swiped his ID badge through the card reader, clocking in. He checked the time. "I'm okay. I'm on the later shift."

"Yeah, I know." Jason peered at him. "You look a little rough. Out all night partying?"

"No, my house guest was up howling."

"Dayum, son, did you get laid?" Jason held up a hand for a fist bump, but Mike ignored it.

"No, I got a cat."

Jason snorted. "Anyway, there was some vandalism over in the Bio Building last night. I'm gonna need your help over there today. I already let the dispatcher know to put your other jobs on a back burner for the time being."

Mike looked up. A fire engine had pulled out of the lot as he'd parked, but he hadn't thought much of it. He'd figured it was just a fire drill in a dorm. "What happened?"

"Somebody trashed one of the labs. It's your girl's place."

Adrenaline spiked through Mike's veins. He barely knew Lauren, but the thought of her in danger made him want to growl. "Is she okay?" He didn't bother to argue that "his girl" wasn't his girl. That was kind of a non-issue under these circumstances.

Jason shrugged. "Cool as a cucumber. I saw her when I went over. She wasn't there when it happened. We got called over to check it out right after I got here, but there wasn't anything we could do until the cops left. Housekeeping's got a big job ahead of them, and a lot of equipment was damaged, so I need you over there to try to figure out what's fixable and what needs to be replaced."

"Damn," Mike said. He grabbed his work phone and clipped it to his belt. He wanted to rush over, make sure Lauren really was okay, but forced himself to slow down. Who would have done this? Someone after her drug?

His stomach clenched. *Dylan.* His little brother had said he'd been working late in the lab with Lauren, which was a lie because Mike had been with her. But maybe Dylan had been alone in the lab, destroying it. Except why tell Mike he was there when he knew the damage would be discovered?

He briefly considered that maybe Lauren herself had done this. Maybe she'd driven away from her bleeding heart animal rescue shelter to destroy expensive equipment in a crazy, savage fit of psychosis. *Yeah, right.*

Every time he wondered about her being part of the Devil's Rangers, his heart gave a weird squeeze. Although he wasn't into self-delusion, he didn't really think that she was involved—hopefully, that was true, and not just because he wanted *her*, in spite of himself. At any rate, he wasn't going to find out anything standing there gathering wool while Jason scratched his armpits. "Okay, I'm heading over there."

. . .

Lauren stood in the doorway of her lab, holding a lab coat and box of gloves that someone had handed to her. She couldn't leave this mess for the housekeeping staff—she needed to find out what was salvageable. And find out if she still had a project.

The cops had come and gone, too, although they'd kept her out of her own lab as they'd processed the scene.

They'd asked her the same questions—*any sign of forced entry?* Nope, the doorframe was completely unscratched. Which was weird, because she was sure she'd locked up before she left last night. *Did she know who would have destroyed her lab?* Nope again. *Who would do something like this? Did she have enemies?* Yeah, riiiiight. She'd almost laughed at that one.

While the police had been there, the other members of the department kept popping by, surprisingly generous with offers of refrigerator and freezer space—commodities that were often jealously hoarded. Evan was the only one who was still physically present, however. Once the police left, there was no more gossip to collect. She sighed and held the box of gloves between her knees while she wrestled her arms into the lab coat. Time to get to work.

Evan handed her a pair of plastic shoe covers. "Here. Wear these. You don't know what's contaminating the floor."

"Thanks."

"Are you okay?" Evan's formal reserve slipped a bit, and he put his hand on her arm. He was a good guy under all that uptight armor, which made her think of his completely-wrong-for-her brother with the mysterious background and dark look in his eye.

"I will be. I just can't believe someone came in here and did this. I can't believe no one saw anything."

"I was here until late," Evan said. "I saw the cleaning people leave, and everything was fine. The perpetrators must have come in during the dead of night."

"Miss Kane?"

Lauren turned to see a man in a Tucker Police Department uniform striding toward her. He was about thirty, African American, with a gleaming shaved head and the height and lean power of someone who hadn't stopped playing basketball after his high school—or maybe even college—career had ended. Of course, she was making an assumption that all incredibly tall guys played ball. His long face was serious, but not unsympathetic.

"I'm Chief of Police Dwayne Crawford," he told her, shaking her hand. "I'm sorry it took me so long to get here." He turned to Evan. "Nice to see you, Evan."

Evan nodded stiffly. "Hello, Chief Crawford."

The man sighed. "Oh, for God's sake, we went to preschool together. You really, *really* don't need to call me 'Chief.'"

Evan almost smiled.

Chief Crawford turned his attention back to her. "This your lab?"

Lauren nodded.

Evan said, "I'll be in my office if you need me."

"Thanks," Lauren said. Then, puzzled by why a police chief would be at her lab, she turned to the police chief. "Since when does the police chief show up at the site of a little vandalism?"

"Tucker's a small force, and we don't get crimes like this often."

He looked over Lauren's shoulder, into the lab. "It looks like you've got a hell of a mess to clean up. Mind if I look around a little with you?"

"I was just gearing up." She handed him some gloves.

"I'd like to see if you can identify anything that might be missing and get an in-person look at the graffiti."

"Graffiti? I don't know anything about that."

"The first responders noticed it, but didn't mention it to anyone because of its threatening nature."

Lauren looked through the door. She was hesitant to take a step over the threshold, as if by staying in the corridor, she could keep the destruction from being real. God, how was she going to replace all this stuff? "I don't see anything. What kind of threats?"

"Not very nice ones," Crawford said.

But before they entered the room, Mike burst through the fire door at the end of the hall, long legs eating the distance between himself and Lauren. He came toward her so quickly that she stepped back, lest he bowl her over, but he pulled up before that happened. She was close enough to feel his energy. A nice little vibration crawled up her back—one that had nothing to do with all the bad stuff that had happened in her lab.

"Are you okay?" His dark brown eyes were nearly black, searching hers. Somehow he was more handsome this morning than he'd been last night. Probably a reaction based on the overflow of stress hormones running through her system. Yeah, that had to be it.

Crawford was covering a smile with his hand. From the corner of her eye, Lauren noticed Evan come to his office door and stare at his brother. What was all that about?

"Um, hi," Lauren said weakly. She found herself leaning slightly forward, wanting to put her hands on his and pull his strong arms around her. *Oh, no.* That wouldn't do. "I'm…I'm okay, I think."

Evan shook his head, turned, and shut the door.

"Crawford," Mike said, turning from her to shake the cop's hand.

"Gibson! It's about time you showed your face. I told Evan you needed to come see me."

"Yeah, I've been pretty busy." Mike said, looking away.

Were they old friends? Enemies? Frienemies? It *was* a small town.

"Uh, huh. Nice outfit, by the way."

Mike didn't respond, but Crawford continued. "I told your brother you should have come to me for a job when you moved back to town. If you want to be back in a blue uniform, I could hook you up in something a little more up your alley." He held up a hand when Mike glowered at him. "Not my business, I know." He looked at Lauren, then back at Mike, who frowned. "What I didn't know was that you're involved with our victim."

"Oh!" Lauren said at the same time Mike said, "Huh?"

"We're not—I mean, there's not—" She stopped and looked at Mike.

"Do you know who did this?" Mike asked Crawford,

not addressing the implication that there was something between himself and Lauren. There wasn't, so that was a reasonable response. Except...God, she was just really glad to see him.

"No clue who did this...yet," Crawford said to Mike. "I was just about to take a look."

Mike hesitated, then said, "I'm supposed to make a list of equipment that needs repair. Should I come back later, or —"

"You might as well come in now."

Lauren was so relieved that Mike was allowed to come in with her that she almost missed the hint of satisfaction that crossed his face.

They pulled on the shoe covers and stepped across the threshold. Everything from the counters in the middle of the room had been tipped to the floor. The shelves above the center benches were likewise knocked over, contents spilled everywhere. The two cubicle desk spaces on the far wall, where the windows overlooked the parking lot, looked like a paper factory had vomited.

The first thing Lauren looked for was her algae, which should have been bubbling happily in its giant flask. But it wasn't. Oh, God. She stifled a gasp with a cough.

"Are you okay?" Crawford asked.

"Um, yeah. I just...yeah, I'm okay." Her algae was gone. The incubation flask was full of pale green liquid, but some- one had taken the time to strain out the organisms. All that was left was...algae pee. She swallowed, hard, hoping against hope that the bag of dried step one algae — and the purified step two liquid — were in the safe. They were not. The door hung open, the safe empty. *Crap*. The story she'd heard on the radio yesterday ran, loud and clear, through her head. *A dangerous new drug…sending addicts to the hospital…* Nausea rolled through her, threatening to bring her to her knees.

She looked up. Crawford was examining something in the cell culture room. Mike stared right at her.

"Dr. Kane, can you come in here?" Chief Crawford asked.

Mike looked away.

With slow steps, she walked to see where Crawford was pointing. When she saw the words written on the wall by the incubator, she nearly threw up.

Chapter Seven

Lauren looked truly green around the gills. Mike watched as Crawford put a hand around Lauren's upper arm and steered her away from the room with the gruesome threat spray painted on the wall. Mike would have rather taken her completely out of the building, somewhere totally safe.

KILLING RATS IS KILLING DOGS IS KILLING MONKEYS IS KILLING SCIENTISTS. ARE YOU NEXT?

Below the words was a squiggle that Mike recognized. He wondered if Lauren or Crawford knew it for the gang tag that it was. Dino Romain and the Devil's Rangers had been here.

"Why would someone say that?" Lauren said, nearly—but not quite—wailing. She was hanging on, but just barely.

"Are you up for some questions?" Crawford asked.

She nodded. "I guess so."

He pulled a notebook, similar to the one Mike still carried everywhere, from his shirt pocket. "Do you know who did this?"

Lauren shook her head. "No. I don't know why…" Her eyes flew to Mike's and then to the safe.

Crawford didn't miss the look. "What do you keep in the safe?"

She sighed. "step two. It's a narcotic, stronger than morphine, produced by genetically altered algae. I change it… run it through a series of purification steps and alter one of the side chains on the main—" she said, then stopped, waved a hand, and started again. "Anyway, I turn it into a benign but powerful painkiller. I call that step three."

"What's step one?"

She gestured toward the giant flask that Mike recalled had been bubbling with dark green slime the day before. Now it held cloudy green water. "I call that step zero. Grow the algae. Then I strain it and dry it, make it into pellets. That's step one. I didn't produce steps zero and one this week."

She was lying. She'd told the truth about the missing vial of step two drug, but both big bags of step one pellets were gone. He knew she'd taken one bag with her the night before…the one she'd probably handed off to the old guy in the dusty Honda, but what about the other bag? There had been two on the counter when she'd been telling him about her research the day before.

For some reason, knowing Lauren was lying about the missing algae didn't set Mike's overdeveloped conscience to DEFCON One. He should tell Crawford that she wasn't being straight, but he didn't. And he didn't think it was because he wanted to bust her as part of the drug ring himself, since he didn't. He'd give it some time.

Crawford scribbled some more notes. "I think you'd better explain the whole process."

While Lauren recited everything she'd said to Mike the day before—but with more detail and bigger words—Mike examined the lab, partially to see what equipment was damaged but mostly to see if he could figure out if Lauren could have trashed her own lab. He needed to know in his heart, to be one hundred and ten percent sure that she was innocent—because she was starting to matter to him. It didn't make sense—she would just take her own stuff out of here, no one would know, no need to make a big mess. But then what was with the meeting last night, passing that stuff off to the old guy in the parking lot at the animal shelter? He had to find some way to casually find out if she'd indeed passed on her pellets to the old dude without triggering her suspicions.

"I know you won't have a complete inventory until you've had time to clean up, but can you tell me anything that's missing?" Crawford asked.

"Just…my step two drug." Lauren met Mike's gaze then, as though daring him to contradict her. But he wouldn't. He wasn't going to call her on her lie just yet. He would wait until Crawford was gone, find out what game she was playing. Yeah, he should probably speak up now, but something—hopefully not his hormones—was telling him to give her a chance.

Meanwhile, he had to be a maintenance man. He made a note to check the freezer to make sure it held its temperature once it got set back upright, then pulled the ultracentrifuge away from the wall to see if he could put the control panel back in or if he needed to call in someone else.

The old guy—Dr. Jerrold—who'd spoken to Evan in the hallway the day before, stuck his head through the door. He dressed like Evan probably would in another fifteen years—if not before. This guy's pants were belted so far over his stomach that the hems were well above the tops of his black socks. Mike conceded to himself that Evan, at least, didn't wear flood pants, and he kept his belt somewhere closer to his actual waist, even if he did wear a purple and green argyle sweater vest.

"Lauren, do you have a minute? I need you to sign some papers for the insurance company." The old guy looked at Crawford. "Your people took pictures? I'll need copies."

Crawford nodded.

As soon as Lauren left the room, Mike approached Crawford and said, in a low voice, "I think you've got some sort of Devil's Rangers connection here."

"Why do you think that?"

Mike just looked at Crawford.

The cop blinked, then said, "That's why you're here, isn't it? They think that Devil's Dust is coming from *here*?"

"Shhh…" Mike looked over his friend's shoulder to the hallway.

Crawford grinned big enough that Mike was afraid he was going to sprain a smile muscle. "I knew it. I knew you didn't do what they said. They just *said* they suspended you so you could come here undercover."

Mike waited a moment, then watched Crawford's face change as he realized the truth.

"No. If you were undercover in an official capacity, I would have been notified." Crawford dragged his hand over his mouth. "They really think you did what they said? You're not guilty though, are you?"

Mike just shrugged.

"I didn't believe it when your old partner—what was his name?"

"Dan."

"Yeah, I didn't believe it when old Dan told me you were dirty, and I don't believe it now." He slapped Mike on the shoulder. "The job offer's still open. And you come see me when you can. I'll do what I can to help."

Mike shook his head. It would be easier to stay below the radar if people like Dwayne believed he was guilty and didn't try to help him. If he couldn't be officially undercover, it was better that he just looked like a low-life ex-cop. That way, when he found the Devil's Dust connection, he wouldn't endanger anyone but himself.

• • •

After signing the insurance papers for Dr. Jerrold, Lauren returned to her lab to try to start the clean up. The police chief asked a few more questions and gave Lauren his card before leaving, telling her to call if she thought of anything else.

All she could think of right now was trying to find out who had stolen her drug and getting it back before the Pemberton Society got wind of her loss. She was supposed to send them five freaking grams of the stuff by next week. She couldn't let Pemberton know that she didn't have the drug, or they'd pull the plug on her funding. She didn't have enough time to grow more by next week. She *had* to find the stuff. Before the police did. Because if the police did find her product, it would go into some evidence locker somewhere until long after the window of the Pemberton opportunity—and Lauren's career—was closed and sealed shut. She would sell a kidney before she called her mother and admitted she couldn't make it in science.

She wasn't sure how she'd find out who the bad guys were, but she'd seen the way Mike's eyes had narrowed when he read the graffiti on the wall, and there was something about the way he talked with Crawford… He knew something. And she was going to find out what it was and how it could help her. And maybe how to get her drug back.

She absolutely had to find that stuff before the police did.

And before anyone died. *Dangerous new drug…addicts to the hospital…* Please, God…don't let it be her drug they were talking about on the news.

After Crawford left, Mike stopped fiddling with settings on the centrifuge. He straightened and turned to lean against a clean section of counter. Crossing his arms, he glared at Lauren.

"What?" She realized she'd crossed her arms, too, and stood with a hip cocked out. Defensive much? "Let's have it."

"You lied."

"About what?"

"What's missing. Those pellet things you showed me yesterday. They're all gone."

Damn.

"Yeah. You wanna start talking?" He uncrossed his arms and moved toward Lauren.

He smelled of fabric softener again, like the day before.

What single guy used fabric softener?

"Are you married?" *Ugh*. Did she really say that?

That slowed him down, though. "What? No. I live with my brother. I told you that last night." He took another step into her personal space. "Why did you lie?"

Instead of feeling intimidated, she found herself uncrossing her arms and putting her hands behind her to hold on to the ledge. "How's the cat doing?"

"Howled all night. Dylan threatened to poison it."

"Dylan did? But he's such an animal lover!"

"Shows you how much of a head case that cat is." He pinned her in place with that dark stare. "Why did you lie?"

He was so close that she could feel his heat. How much closer was he going to get?

When she took a deep breath, her breasts brushed his chest. Which caused her to take another deep breath. Not on purpose, of course.

His eyes heated. She could smell coffee now. She licked her lips, and his nostrils flared. He bent his head closer.

She needed to answer his question, but what should she say? If she didn't answer, would he…what, kiss it out of her? He should work for the CIA. Or the FBI. As part of the Threaten to Kiss Information From Witnesses Unit.

This couldn't happen. She didn't have room for a guy in her life under the best circumstances, and right now, she needed to find her drug. How was she going to do that if she had her lips stuck to his? Those gorgeous, sexy lips that probably had magnets in them. Magnets for desperate and dateless science geek girl lips. "I have to find the algae before the police do. I have to get it back so I can make enough step three to send to the drug company that I'm hoping will fund my study. My entire career hangs on getting this money. Without the algae…" Well, she guessed, the truth was always an option.

He blinked and stepped back, saying nothing.

She felt strangely sad that he hadn't had to resort to more drastic measures to get her to talk. He was awfully interested in this situation. And why had Crawford seemed to want Mike there while he examined the crime scene? "Why do you care so much about this?"

Mike retreated to the other side of the aisle and crossed his arms again. "Does my brother have a key to your lab? Can he get in here after hours?"

"Dylan?" Lauren tilted her head. *Ah.* She supposed that, if she had a brother, and he worked somewhere there had been such chaos, she'd be a little freaked out too, but… "No. I mean, yes, he has a key, but I don't think he did this, and I can't believe you do."

"I didn't say I did. But someone did. What did you give that man at the animal shelter last night?"

"Huh?" *What the…?* "Oh! Rick. It was rat food. Why do you want to know…" A lightbulb in her brain went on.

The rat food pellets were in a bag just like the one she kept the algae in. Mike had been in the parking lot when she'd come out of the building last night. She'd dropped the bag and nearly fallen down the stairs when she saw him looking at her, and he must have recognized it. Had he followed her to the shelter to see what she was going to do with the pellets? But why? Realization hit, and hard. Oh, God. Well, that cleared up one mystery. He hadn't followed her out there because he was interested in her in that way. He probably didn't have magnets in his lips, either.

"You don't think *I* had anything to do with this, do you?" She held up a hand when he opened his mouth to speak, so he snapped it shut. "Are you a cop?"

He didn't answer, just stared at her for a moment longer. He chewed his bottom lip, apparently having some sort of an internal debate.

"Dr. Kane, do you—" Evan burst through the door. "Oh. Sorry. I didn't realize you were still here. I saw Crawford leaving, so I figured—"

"Evan." Mike nodded and picked up his tool bag and slung it over his shoulder. He looked at Lauren. "I've got to get a report back to my boss with a time estimate for the work in here. Call the maintenance department with a list. We'll get started as soon as possible, and I'll help you take care of this."

She had a feeling he was talking about more than her broken equipment. And she knew, quite clearly, he'd completely avoided answering her question. Did that mean he *was* a cop? But if he was, why was he here, on campus? Investigating what?

After Mike walked out the door, Evan turned to Lauren and said, "You need to stay away from him."

"Excuse me?"

Evan took a deep breath, then let it out. "I'm a bit concerned that my brother is spending so much time here, at the scene of a crime."

"He came to find out what needs to be fixed." Why was she defending Mike's presence when she'd just been questioning it, herself? "He's helping me."

"Of course." He nodded, though clearly *not* agreeing with her. "And...I understand the effect that so much testosterone has on the female libido, and the 'bad boy' phenomenon probably amplifies that, but—although it seems disloyal of me to say so—Michael has had some issues—some trouble that I shouldn't discuss with you—from the past."

Before he could continue, Lauren asked, "Did you need something specific, Evan?"

"Oh. I wanted to know if you're coming to the departmental seminar. It starts in"—he pulled back the cuff of his perfectly pressed oxford cloth shirt—"three minutes."

"I think I'll skip it today. I doubt anyone will think badly of me."

"Well, I won't, but you know that Dr. Jerrold does take faculty attendance, even if it's not officially recorded.

"Thanks Evan. I'll take my chances." She was pretty sure that she could get away with missing a meeting. Besides, in addition to trying to salvage her project and save her career, she had to worry about what kind of "issues" Evan was talking about. Well, no, she didn't *have* to worry about that. She *could* just avoid Mike Gibson and get on with saving her own career. But she had a feeling that he was going to take up a good bit of space in her brain, whether she wanted him there or not. And besides, she had a feeling that he held a key to getting her algae back.

Chapter Eight

Lauren spent a few more hours fending off well-meaning co-workers who came by to offer their theories about the crime. It took every stiff-upper-lip gene imparted by her parents not to snap, but she didn't lose her mind at anyone who leaned against a counter and offered advice.

Aaaand then, her mother called. Lauren was hoping she wouldn't have to tell her parents what happened until she knew more—and maybe had her algae back. No such luck. She'd learned long ago not to ignore a call from Karen Kane. The woman was nothing if not persistent.

It only took Lauren fifteen minutes and half a box of tissues to get herself under control enough to get back to work after telling her mom that she'd had a liiiiiittle setback on the road to scientific glory.

But she never did get a single beaker back on its proper shelf that afternoon.

She probably would have made more progress, but she

kept getting distracted with worries about how to find her missing drug. She did manage to clean her algae tank and get it up and running again. Fortunately, it didn't require any sophisticated equipment — just a jug of nutrient-rich water and some UV light. Barring a working grow light, a sunny window would do, which was what she placed the tank under.

Sunshine through a north-facing window wasn't going to be enough to dig her out of her step one deficit, however. It took a week — under optimal conditions — to grow enough raw material to harvest the step one algae, dry it into pellets, and extract it into the potent, liquid step two substance, another few days to process it into step three — the chemical she hoped to use to launch herself into pharmaceutical history. And her meeting with the Pemberton society was in five days.

And she'd tried to avoid thinking about this, but she was really beginning to be bugged about that news story she'd heard yesterday. What if that Devil's Dust crap was her drug? She'd been noticing a shortage in her step two production. Could someone have possibly been siphoning off the drug as it dripped from the condenser, even before the lab was sacked and robbed?

She mentally reviewed the production steps. After she grew algae in the flasks, she strained it out, mixed in the toxic chemical that would cause it to release the drug later, and dried it into pellets, which she kept until she had enough to process. Then, she mixed the pellets with extraction solution and put them in another set of flasks with a condenser. The step two drug dripped out of the condenser. For every liter of extraction, she should get ten milliliters of step two. And she did. She got the ten milliliters, anyway. But not as much concentrated step two as she had the first several times she'd run the experiment. Could someone be taking step two and replacing it with extraction solution?

Who would know how to do that? Maybe someone who had heard one of her seminars, when she'd presented her data. But as she thought about the members of the Biology Department, she couldn't imagine a single one of them taking her drug. Who would even know how to sell it to bad guys?

She had to find out who had her drug and get it back. But how?

Put an ad in the paper? Drug dealers probably didn't read the paper. For that matter, regular people didn't read the paper anymore. Craigslist? Make a plea on the news, like parents who'd lost a child? Tacky, at best. Hire a posse of mercenaries?

At this last thought, Lauren started to giggle. She envisioned herself wearing camo, striding back and forth in front of a group of former Navy SEALs, giving them a speech about the dangers of drugs and the necessity of developing safe alternatives.

The one thing she couldn't do was tell the police that she had to get her drug back. If they knew she was going to try to get to the stuff before they got their hands on it, they wouldn't tell her anything about the progress of the investigation. Heck, they'd probably suspect her. But Mike had some sort of connection to Chief Crawford.

And what about Mike? Should she avoid him, like Evan suggested? Lauren was bummed about that. Way more than she should have been after knowing the man all of what? Thirty-some hours? Her instincts said that she should get closer to him, find out what he knew—but she thought perhaps that was her girly parts' influence on her instincts and not her rational brain.

At six thirty, Lauren finally gave up trying to work. She'd forgotten to eat lunch, and was getting a whale of a headache. She needed to get home and feed her cat, then call Crawford and find out if he'd made any progress. Because he would *totally* appreciate that. She should also try to sleep, because if she couldn't figure out where her missing drug had ended up, she'd be forced to stay in the lab all weekend, trying to resurrect at least something of her research. She might go down in flames if she couldn't secure the Pemberton grant, but she wouldn't go down without fighting.

As she walked to her car in the slanting evening sunshine, the trash can where the possum family lived caught her attention. There was a sign taped to the can.

DO NOT DISTURB. THIS TRASH CAN IS SOMEONE'S HOME.

There was also a little barrier of cinder blocks and caution tape in place, presumably to slow anyone who might not stop to read the sign before tossing in something that might cause traumatic brain injury to little, innocent possum babies.

Mike.

In her mind's eye, she could see him out here, building a little safety zone, and her girly parts sent another zing to her instincts, telling her to trust him.

But then there was all that stuff Evan had said.

Would someone with the mysterious *issues* that Evan mentioned spend time to ensure the protection of a family of scavengers? And adopt a special needs cat? And would he make Lauren's heart beat harder just from being in the same room? Of course, even Dr. Evil had that little hairless thing he seemed to care for.

"They seem to be doing pretty well."

Lauren jumped at the sound of Mike's voice.

"How did you sneak up on me?"

"Sorry," he said, putting a hand on her arm to steady her. Where he touched her, her skin tingled. "You seemed to be deep in thought."

"Uh…" She wondered if he could tell that she'd been thinking of him. The way her cheeks burned, he probably suspected as much. After all, he was pretty good at suspecting things, and at asking questions.

Screw it. She had to know. "Are you a cop? Or *were* you? Why did Evan say you've been in trouble? And why are you still here? Shouldn't you have been off work hours ago?" And, yes, she was rambling now, throwing questions at him faster than he could answer, but it was all out now, and she had no choice but to see how he responded.

Mike sighed, letting go of her arm. He ran a hand through his hair. Finally, he said, "I was a member of an interstate police task force, and…there was a…misunderstanding, and now I'm a maintenance man. And I'm still on campus, because I had some…extra stuff to do today."

She wondered what that might be. Former police guy working as a maintenance man where a probably drug-related crime had been committed?

He looked away, then back at her. "And, uh, I was waiting for you."

"What do they say you did? That got you fired?" She was going to ignore the "waiting for you" part of that statement, because she couldn't process that right now.

"It's complicated." He shook his head, then smiled, wryly. "And I was 'suspended indefinitely', not fired."

Lauren crossed her arms and regarded him. "Of course it's complicated. But I'm pretty quick on the draw. Try me."

For a split second, his glance dropped—to her lips? His pocket chimed with an incoming text sound, and he took his phone out and glanced at it before shoving it back. "Look, I'd better run. I just wanted to make sure you're okay."

He'd waited there, after a long day, just to make sure she was okay? His eyes searched hers. Looking for…what? To see if she was going to hand off drugs disguised as rat food to a friend or for something more…personal? Whatever it was he was looking for, she felt like she could give it to him, and it would be safe. Suddenly, the events of the day swamped her, and she sagged, shoulders slumping.

"Damn," he said, took a step forward, and pulled her into his arms.

She was shocked, in a good, swirly rush kind of a way. Tentatively, she reached around his waist and clung, just for a moment. Okay, maybe two moments. Two and a half. The heat and pressure of his body against hers were comforting and arousing in equal measures. And he had back muscles. *Latissimus dorsi*, originating right under her fingers. She bet if she let her hands travel, his *rectus abdomini* were even more adapted to supporting her fingers.

Before she could start drooling and reviewing anatomy by Braille, she released him. He let her go and stepped back.

That big hand was in his hair again, pushing it off of his forehead. "Okay. Umm…I guess…" He didn't meet her eyes right away, and then he did.

She tried not to drown in the dark pools. Clearing her

throat, she said, "Okay, well, thanks. You know, for…coming to the lab today. And for taking care of the possums. And for hugging me."

He smiled. "You betcha. Have a good night." He turned and walked away, the early fall evening shadows stretching away from him, as tall as Superman could leap.

Damn. She had even less understanding of what was going on, but found that the likelihood of getting away from Mike Gibson without her feelings involved was slipping.

• • •

Mike sat in his parked truck to watch his house for a few minutes before going inside. Dylan's silhouette moved behind the kitchen curtains, confirming the text he'd gotten a few minutes ago telling Mike he'd meet him at home. The kid was probably microwaving something from the frozen pizza department. He needed to confront Dylan about what had happened in Lauren's lab, but he needed to sit there and avoid the confrontation for a few minutes first. He went back over the events of the day, from hearing about the damage, to finding the Devil's Rangers gang tag on the lab wall, his inability to get any information about the Rangers from his old co-workers, to seeing Lauren outside of the biology building.

He'd meant to ask more questions when he'd seen Lauren outside of the lab, to see if he could figure out who—hopefully, not Dylan—might have been hanging around her lab. Someone who would know what to steal. He knew she wasn't responsible for the drug thefts. She'd explained about the bag of pellets she'd taken from the building last night, and it was a dumb enough story that he believed it. He even understood why she hadn't told Crawford about the missing algae pellets. She had no reason to trash her own lab—unless she was completely bent, and he didn't get that kind of vibe—but truthfully, he had little objectivity where she was concerned. And Dylan had access to all of it.

Still. Why did he have to go and fucking *hug* her? What was wrong with him? She'd just looked so…vulnerable, after her cool competence when he'd gone into the lab with her earlier. *Fuck*.

He couldn't get attached to her. He didn't do relationships. Relationships came with responsibilities, and he already had enough to distract him from his work. He got out of the truck and slammed the door. It *thunked* shut on the first try for a change. He hoped that was a good sign.

Through the kitchen door window, he could see Dylan bent over his phone, leaning against the counter. The door screeched when he pulled it open, and Dylan's head whipped up. He punched the blackout button on the screen and shoved it into his pocket, then hooked his fingers in his belt.

"S'up," Dylan said, nodding.

"Hey. Did you eat?" Mike asked. That was neutral. Good start.

"Yeah." Dylan jerked his head toward the stove, where the leftover half of a formerly frozen pizza sat. "That's from yesterday, I just re-nuked it. I'm done, help yourself."

Mike took a slice, holding it with one hand while he opened the refrigerator and took out a Diet Coke with the other. He deftly popped the tab and sucked down half of the soda, trying to figure out how to ask his brother if he was doing drugs. Or dealing them. Or both. "Where's the cat?"

"Hiding behind the dryer, last time I checked."

"Seriously? How does it fit?"

Dylan shrugged. "You've got something you want to say to me?"

Was he that obvious? Mike shoved half the slice into his mouth, chewed maybe all of three times, then swallowed. Grandma would kick him in the shin if she could see him right now. Standing up to eat and choking down store-bought pizza. Grandma would also know how to talk to Dylan. If she were still here, Mike wouldn't even need to have this conversation, because his brother never would have gotten into trouble in the first place.

Dylan waited, defensive shields up and ready to deflect. When Dylan reached up to scratch his neck, his shirt gaped at the waist. Mike caught a glimpse of the scar that he knew extended from his brother's collarbone to his belly. Appetite gone, he threw the rest of the slice of pizza in the trash.

Dylan watched him but didn't say anything. He probably knew how reminders of that scar, and Mike's role in it, made Mike feel.

"You know what happened at your boss's lab overnight?" Mike asked, deliberately shifting the conversation.

Dylan nodded. "I heard about it."

"Do you know how it happened?"

"Don't you mean, 'Did you do it?'"

Yes. "No, I mean, do you know anything about it?"

Dylan sighed. "I know that someone broke in and trashed the place. I heard that some chemicals were stolen, and that the police are questioning everyone with access to the Biology building. Including students and maintenance staff." At the last, Dylan raised an eyebrow at Mike.

"I've already talked to the police."

"Well. Are you sure *you* aren't involved?"

Mike took a breath, let it out slowly. This wasn't working. He wouldn't learn anything about Dylan by talking to Dylan.

He could pump Evan for information, but Evan didn't trust Mike any more than Dylan did. He was just going to have to watch and listen. But he was going to be watching like a hawk with a satellite hookup.

First, he had to try one more thing. "There was graffiti on the wall of that room your boss uses for growing her algae."

"The cell culture room?"

"Whatever. There was a weird threat about killing things, but that's not what struck me."

"No? Please share."

Mike walked over to Dylan and flicked up the sleeve of his T-shirt, revealing the tattoo that he had yet to have removed.

Dylan jerked away, but not before Mike tapped him right in the middle of the Devil's Rangers gang tag inked into his brother's skin.

Dylan's expression was a mixture of fear and revulsion. "Dude. I didn't do this. I swear. Dr. Kane is awesome. I *wouldn't* do this."

Mike wanted to believe his brother. He wanted to believe him so much that he could have cried. But he couldn't ignore the evidence. Lauren's face flashed through his consciousness, along with the feel of her in his arms.

He tossed the Diet Coke in the sink and replaced it with a beer.

Chapter Nine

Saturday morning, Lauren put her giant mug of Earl Grey tea on the little table outside the lab and wondered for a moment if that was a good idea. *'Cause you never know when someone's going to walk by and spike your drink with radioactive thymidine while you worked.* Nothing like some senseless vandalism to turn up the paranoia to eleven.

The double door at the end of the hallway clanged, and Lauren looked up to see Dylan White clumping down the hall. "Dylan!" He'd never just shown up out of the blue before, and especially on a weekend. Weren't college kids supposed to be sleeping off hangovers on early Saturday mornings? "What brings you here?"

The young man ducked his head. "I feel bad that I didn't come by yesterday. I had a…thing…and I got caught up in that."

"That's okay. It wasn't your day to work anyway." She looked at him closely, trying to find a resemblance to Evan or Mike. There was something about their eyes, a sort of tilt to the eyelids, maybe. Dylan also had the same straight blade of a nose, but it was still too big for his face. And he had that ridiculous chinstrap beard. He'd grow into the nose, but the beard? Hopefully, he'd outgrow that.

"What?" he asked.

"Nothing. Yesterday was kind of crazy, anyway. I take it you heard—"

"Yeah, I heard. That's really fu—messed up." Dylan hiked up his baggy plaid shorts and grimaced. "I should have been here to help yesterday. But maybe I can work today and help you out?"

"Well—"

"We don't even have to put it on my timecard if you don't want. I just thought…"

He looked so earnest, with his big brown eyes and even bigger nose, that Lauren's heart—already pretty mushy when it came to Dylan—melted a little more. "Well then, strap on a lab coat and glove up. Maybe you can show me how this computer tracing GPS app thing that IT put on my laptop is supposed to work."

"They did that for my computer when they set me up with a campus log on," he said. "Is your laptop here?"

"It's at home, but the tracking program is on my desktop over there," she said, waving in the general vicinity of her desk. "And on my phone. My scientific competence doesn't extend to computer literacy." A fact that Alex the Ex had mentioned on more than…a dozen occasions.

"My computer skills are second only to my ability to scrape algae off test tubes, and equally at your service," he said with a flourish and a bow.

Lauren laughed. He was a good kid.

When he entered the room, he brought with him some sort of too-piney-too-sandalwoody whirlwind of scent, and she sneezed.

"Uh oh," Dylan said.

"What is that? A new cologne?"

"Yeah." His cheeks were red. "It's called Rebel Max. It's supposed to have women falling over themselves to get close to me."

"Um…" She sneezed again.

"I guess I need to stay downwind of the ladies, or they're going to be falling over themselves to get away."

How to be diplomatic? "Um…maybe you should work over by the fume hood, so the smell gets sucked out by the ventilation system."

Once they found a configuration where Dylan's cologne didn't send Lauren into anaphylactic shock, they got busy putting the lab to rights. Working for an hour or so, they chatted about television shows and YouTube videos. At about six-feet-two and about a hundred and sixty pounds, Dylan shocked Lauren when he told her he'd be playing rugby in the spring. Not only was the kid way too skinny for that kind of a contact sport, he seemed a little too—hip, or cool, or something—to go out for a gritty sport like rugby.

"Wow, that sounds…challenging," she finally said.

"You're too nice. My brother's words were 'bleeping stupid as bleep.'"

Lauren wanted to know about Mike's relationship with Dylan—and Evan for that matter—but she didn't know how to ask without sounding like she was fishing. Which she was. Which she shouldn't be, because she had no business thinking about Mike Gibson under any circumstance.

Well, except that he'd hugged her last night. And sort of, maybe, almost kissed her the night before that, in front of the animal shelter. That moved their relationship to some sort of level above "just met," she figured. Not that she should be figuring out anything to do with her and Mike.

What she *needed* to figure out was how the heck she was going to get her algae back.

While Dylan went to check on some items that he'd put in the autoclave, Lauren's cell phone rang. She checked the caller ID, saw that it was from the animal rescue group, took the call, then spent the next ten minutes trying to pay attention as she was relayed the sad life story of a recently deceased race horse and the miniature pig that had been its companion. The pig was in mourning after the death of its horse friend and wasn't getting along with the other pigs that it was being fostered with. She was needed to drive the pig to a new home in Ohio.

When Dylan walked back into the room, she was desperately trying to explain why she couldn't drive a pig around various counties on a Saturday. She broke off when Dylan waved at her, trying to tell her something.

"I can do it," Dylan told her. "If you don't mind me driving your SUV."

"Are you sure? It's a good forty-five minutes each direction."

"No prob. Just give me directions." When she nodded, he took his phone from his pocket and started madly hitting buttons, then stepped into the hall.

Lauren got the details from Lee and followed Dylan out to give him the Post-it with information on it.

"Can't you make up a story?" Dylan was saying, then

suddenly, as if realizing he was no longer alone, added, "Okay, gotta go. See you in a few."

"Everything okay?" Lauren asked, sneezing again when she got near him.

"Uh, yeah," Dylan said. "It's cool if my friend rides along with me, isn't it?"

"Sure, as long as you remember to roll the windows down to air it out when you're done. The pig smell probably won't bother me as much as that cologne."

Dylan left with Lauren's keys, and she went back to sorting slides. Unfortunately, the work was boring enough that her mind wandered into dangerous territory, and she found herself thinking about Mike. Again.

About that hug last night. About how the hard planes of his chest had felt against her softer self. Biologically, she knew that the contrasts between men and women—the mass of male pectoral muscles and female breast tissue—had different evolutionary origins, but she had to wonder if maybe God had thrown some of that hard/soft, strong/gentle business in there as part of the magnetic force that drew opposites together. *Argh*. Again, with the magnets.

She wasn't sure, mostly because she wasn't good at this stuff or had a lot of empirical data with which to compare, but she kind of thought Mike felt the same pull she did. There wasn't any room in her life for a relationship—part of it was that her career was too time-consuming right now, but it was more about the fact that he was a little too...too large and in charge, with the potential to suck the life out of her ambition. But boy, she was enjoying the heck out of imagining what it would be like to be with him, to ignore all the reasons she shouldn't.

. . .

Mike clenched his fingers tightly around the steering wheel of his F-150 as he drove toward campus. He'd been on the computer at his house all morning, trying to Google "fake heroin," "Dino Romain," "Devil's Dust," and "Tucker University," and had gotten nowhere. No connections were on the internet, but that didn't mean there *wasn't* a connection. After slapping the laptop shut, he'd gone to wake up Dylan and get him to help give Possum her morning pill, only to realize the kid wasn't there. Instead, on the floor in Dylan's room was a note saying he'd gone off to work.

Yeah, right. On a Saturday. At least he'd already dosed the cat.

So Mike did what he did best—hit the streets on the hunt for information—and headed over to Tucker U. He wanted to find out what was happening in Lauren's lab, and wanted to know what the hell his little brother was up to. He'd lain awake far too long the night before, trying to come up with a good reason for Dylan to have lied about being in the lab with Lauren the night before the destruction. And then he just thought about Lauren.

Damn.

Feeling her soft curves against his body yesterday, even though it was just a moment... No wonder he couldn't sleep last night.

He parked, noticing Lauren's SUV in the lot next to Dylan's car. Was that good or bad that both of them were there? Seeing Lauren was a distraction...but she also might have information he could use, especially if Crawford was in communication with her. Mike couldn't contact Crawford, but he could talk to Lauren. See what she'd been told by the local police. He stepped out of his truck into the late morning sunshine just in time to see Dylan drive out of the parking lot in Lauren's SUV. *What the—?*

"Hey!" he called, but Dylan either couldn't—or chose not to—hear him. He tried calling the kid's cell phone, to ask where the hell he thought he was going, but his call went straight to voicemail.

Dylan had no business driving her car. No business driving *anyone's* car. The kid was on probation. Getting caught could send him back to jail.

Blood boiling, Mike stormed across the green to Lauren's building, then had to scan his access card three times before the door opened. He strode down the hall, then swung open the door to Lauren's lab.

Her head jerked up at the sound, and she nearly knocked whatever she was working on off of the counter. "What on earth is wrong?"

"What the *fuck* is Dylan doing in your vehicle?"

Lauren put the slide box down and stood, fisted her hands on her hips, and faced him. "Good morning, Mike. Nice to see you." She turned her back to him and wrote something in a notebook.

He came into the lab, undeterred by her deliberate attempt to point out his rudeness. He strode to where she stood. "Where did Dylan go in your car?"

"Is there some emergency that prevents you from asking nicely?"

Okay. He was being an asshole. But he only backed up half a step. Just far enough to cross his arms so that he didn't accidentally smack her in the head when he moved. The smell of her shampoo took some of the wind out of his spinnaker, although he still vibrated with tension. "Good morning, Dr. Kane. Might you be so kind as to tell me where my brother—who is on probation and only supposed to drive to work and school—is going in your vehicle?"

"What?" Her pen clattered onto the counter. "What's he on probation for?" She pushed Mike away and walked halfway across the room before stopping. She looked through the window to the parking lot, as though someone out there would be holding a sign, explaining things to her.

"Didn't you already know this?"

"No. Why should I?"

"Because he works for you."

"He's a student worker. He walked in here and asked for a job, and I told our business office to put him on my grant. We don't run the kids' fingerprints through IAFIS to clean algae tanks."

"Does he have a key to your lab?"

"No," she said slowly.

"No?"

"Um...I've let him have mine a few times, when I couldn't be here and needed him to do some work." She paused, and her mouth opened, shut, then she said, "You can't possibly think he did all this! Besides, I keep the dried algae and the step two drug locked up."

He looked at the safe, closed up now, but it had been hanging open yesterday. "Does he have the combination?"

"No?"

Mike waited.

She sighed. "I keep it written down on a sticky note in

the top drawer of my desk. But I've never taken it out and said, 'Look, here's the combination to the safe.' I have no idea how the bad guys got that open. And the bad guys don't include Dylan."

He didn't want to do this, but she clearly didn't have a clue. "Last year, right after he turned eighteen, he got arrested for vandalism." There was more, a lot more, but Mike couldn't tell her the rest of it without having to explain his own actions, and he wasn't interested in showing her his dirty laundry.

"What? How did that happen?"

The obvious answer—*he went somewhere he wasn't supposed to be, and there was serious collateral damage*—didn't seem to be what she was looking for. So Mike gave her the other answer. Part of the real answer. "I left him alone too much after our Grandma died, and he joined a gang."

"A gang? In Tucker?" She stared at him.

"No, Cincinnati. He lived with me at the time, right after our grandmother died, and I was…involved in some pretty heavy undercover work. I wasn't home much." Jesus, he hated talking about this shit, but her huge eyes seemed to be sucking the truth out of him. Pretty soon he was going to be spilling the whole messed up thing, all the way back to when Mike nearly got Dylan killed.

"What about Evan? Where was— Oh, I remember. He was in Central America."

Mike nodded. Yep, Grandma had died while Evan was in the rainforest collecting frogs, and by the time Mike was able to get him a message, she was buried. Mike hadn't asked Evan to come home and take on part of the responsibility for their brother. All things considered, Mike wasn't sure Evan could have handled things any better, but at least he could have kept Dylan out of the city. Hell, he'd let her house sit empty for all that time, he could have moved them back here sooner.

Lauren seemed to come to some sort of a conclusion then, because she nodded. "Well, he seems to be doing pretty well now. And he's on a mission of mercy, so we'll consider this a work-related outing and not turn him in, huh?"

"I can't wait to hear this explanation," Mike said, leaning back on the bench. "And it had better be good. Because if he's back to his old tricks, I'll take my baby brother to the station myself."

Chapter Ten

"He went to see a pig about a horse."

When Mike laughed, Lauren's heart did one of those little fluttery things she was getting used to feeling when he was around. She loved to see him laugh, she realized with a start. This wasn't a giant gut-grabbing guffaw, but a head-tilting bark of laughter. It turned his throat—and that little shadowy area under his jaw—into somewhere she wanted to lick.

"You know what?" he said. "I actually believe you." He stood there for a second, smiling at her.

Lauren smiled back. *Oh boy.* She liked him. Like, *liked* him. If her best friend had been there, she'd have slipped her a note to pass to Mike, asking if he liked her back. *Check yes or no.*

Then what he had said sunk in and she said, "Wait—why *wouldn't* you believe me?"

"Well…"

She waved the question away. "So what brings you here on a Saturday?"

"I'm on call. I *got* a call, so I came in to fix a leaky sink… and to check up on Dylan. And find out if you've heard an update from Crawford."

Lauren hesitated a minute, then said, "I think it's time for you to tell me your story. There's some kind of…*something* swimming below the surface here."

Mike's gaze narrowed on her mouth.

She licked her lips, but then said, "Oh, no, you're not going to distract me. Spill it."

He raised an eyebrow, and she realized she'd revealed too much—that she was aware of him, of how much he appealed to her. He smirked, then chewed on his bottom lip, as though trying to decide how much to tell her.

Staring straight at her, he said, "I…resigned…because I let a drug dealer get away with a few thousand dollars' worth of heroin."

He looked away then, far away. After a moment, he continued. "We went to make a bust. We'd heard a drug exchange between an out-of-state distributor and a local gang, the Devil's Rangers, was going down in this old factory that was about to be demolished. So we went to bust both the unknown out-of-state distributor and the gang leader, Dino Romain, and whatever lackeys Dino had dragged along. I got to the meet, hid behind a Dumpster, and Romain came in with a couple of his gang members. The problem was, one of the other guys was Dylan."

Lauren couldn't hold in her gasp. Wow. Dylan, a drug-dealing gang member?

Mike nodded. "I almost let him go through with it. I was

so pissed off at him. But I knew he was only there because he was trying to impress Dino—the dumbass had joined the gang to impress Dino's sister. Going to jail would have gotten Dylan killed—brother of a cop, you know. I'd already fucked him up enough—" He took a breath before continuing. "When he came through the door, I grabbed him, slammed him up against a wall. And gave Dino time to snag the dope and get away.

Lauren didn't know what to say. "I have a hard time seeing Dylan involved with drug dealers."

Mike laughed harshly. "It was more about being hot for the drug dealer's mature-beyond-her-years sister."

"Ah."

"It still got him in trouble. Both of us, actually."

"Why were *you* in trouble?"

His mouth had an ironic twist when he said, "Well, there was the small matter of all that heroin walking away from the crime scene. And the mid-level Devil's Ranger that we did manage to bust tried to turn informant by sharing that I had a family connection to the Devil's Rangers. That I turned a blind eye to their drug deals. My boss didn't like me anyway—I had, uh, dated his niece—so he agreed not to prosecute me and to lower the charges against Dylan, but told me I had to go on 'indefinite suspension pending investigation of an ethical violation.'"

"That sounds like made-up bullshit," Lauren said.

He shrugged. "I needed to get Dylan the hell out of that town."

So why didn't you get a job somewhere else?"

"I did. Here."

"I mean as a cop."

Mike shrugged. "If I were to officially resign and go somewhere else, I'd never have a chance to take those sons of bitches down and get my reputation back. Besides, I couldn't bail on Dylan. He's an adult, but he's had it rough — and as much as he hates me…"

"You're family."

He snorted. "For what that's worth. Evan helped get Dylan into Tucker University so the kid would be out of the city and away from the gang. Then this Devil's Dust shit hit the streets, and I hear that it's coming from Tucker U, and that the Devil's Rangers crew is distributing it."

"Did your old coworkers tell you about the Tucker U link?"

He snorted. "They only talk to me on special occasions. Nah, I happened to call my old partner, Dan, a few nights after my suspension hearing when he was three-quarters of the way through a twelve pack, and he, uh, shared his feelings with me. To the tune of, if I hadn't fucked up and let Dino Romain go, this new shit wouldn't be out there putting junkies in even more danger than normal."

"So you think this Devil's Dust is my step two drug?"

He nodded. "Yep. I think that's what the vandalism to your lab was about. To steal your step two."

She sat down on a stool. She'd known she wasn't getting as much step two from her extraction process as she should, and now that a whole lot of it was stolen, was willing to consider the possibility that someone could have been stealing smaller amounts for a while. But having Mike put it out there like this, that her life's work had become a street drug called Devil's Dust, which could *kill* people?? Now she had even more motivation to find those pellets. She had to get them out of circulation—if someone knew how to come into her lab and funnel off product without her knowledge, they could possibly have the skill set to make the step one pellets into step two and make enough Devil's Dust to get every addict in America high. They would need her notes, though. They would need to know how to mix the algae with the toxin that released the drug into the extraction liquid and how to clear out the toxin later.

Fortunately, her notes were safely at home, in her computer and tucked away under her bed, along with dust bunnies and probably a half dozen mismatched socks.

Mike took a step toward her. "So that's the whole story. I've got to find that drug and get these assholes busted, and Tucker University is the best place to do that from."

Lauren considered this. If she kept an eye on Mike, she might be able to get the pellets back before the police could get to them. And Mike was here right now. And very watchable. She focused on the center of Mike's chest, where his faded Tuck U T-shirt had a tiny pinhole. "You're a good guy."

"Not so much." His eyes dropped to her mouth, then back to meet her gaze.

He stared at her. They were standing very close. Well within each other's personal space. His dark brown eyes had little spots of green. And he'd cut himself shaving that morning, because there was a tiny nick on his jaw, halfway between his chin and his ear. And his lips were just the right—something—for his face.

His head had somehow gotten closer to hers. And her body had somehow gotten closer to his. Just before their lips met, she could have sworn she heard him sigh, but that might have been her.

It was a soft, quiet kiss, that much more startling for its gentleness from this big, rough man. No big clacking together of positive and negative poles—a simple brush of lips, but more than that. Something that had been building between them for two days now, ever since she'd tripped over him on her way out of the building.

He started to pull back, so Lauren leaned forward, following him. She pressed her lips to his, more firmly this time, and touched his lower lip with her tongue. He tasted like coffee and peppermint. Her hands moved up his arms to his shoulders, solid under her touch.

He lifted his head from hers then, staring down at her, his expression as shocked as hers must be.

"I'm sorry," he said. "I shouldn't—"

"Why—"

"This isn't—"

He wasn't interested in her *that way*. How embarrassing. "Oh. God, I'm sorry," Lauren said, pushing off of him. She must have caught him off guard, because he stumbled back a step, bumping into the big metal shelving unit behind him.

The top shelf collapsed with a deafening crash, and several large glass and plastic containers of chemicals fell to the ground and shattered, spilling their contents in waves of color and texture. Another tipped over on the top shelf, raining a blinding cloud of powder, coating them both from head to toe.

Lauren started to wipe at her face before she realized that she had no idea what she was about to grind into her skin. Panic set in, injecting epinephrine into her bloodstream in a searing rush. It could be something as benign as table salt—or any number of lethal chemicals that normally lived safely on those shelves. She kept her mouth closed and made a "Mmmph!" sound at Mike. She took his hand and pulled him toward the hall.

They needed to get this washed off before it maybe killed them.

• • •

A soon as Mike saw the powder on Lauren's face, he realized he was in trouble. He needed to jump into action, but he had no idea what he was trying to save her from. Instead, he had to follow her into the hall. She looked a little freaked out, but in control. Her lips were tightly shut, so he kept his mouth closed, too.

She led him to the nearest chemical shower and pulled the chain. After a brief hesitation, the pipe squealed, and water dripped from the oversized showerhead, slowly increasing to a steady flow. Lauren nudged him forward, but when he realized her intent, he grabbed her, yanked her under the water with him, and made sure her face was rinsed off first.

After a few seconds, Lauren stuck out her tongue and tasted the water that poured over her face. She smiled and raised her hands to push her wet hair out of her face.

"Sodium phosphate," she told him. "Totally safe."

They took turns rinsing. When she nodded, Mike pulled the "off" lever. Most of the water made it into the drain under the shower, but there was a decent-size puddle extending around their feet.

As Lauren stepped away from the mess, her foot slid. Mike caught her and pulled her against him before she hit the ground. He held her slender upper arms in his hands, felt soft wet skin under his rough touch.

He knew he should let go, but he couldn't seem to release her. He'd made one mistake by kissing her, and he was probably about to make another.

Lauren leaned back, looking up at Mike. Her golden brown eyes wide. "Oh my God. For a minute there, I had visions of melting like the Wicked Witch of the West." She started to laugh, the sound maybe a little hysterical, and buried her face in his shoulder. She clutched his shirtfront, her breasts pressed against his chest. Hmmm, she must be cold. But *he* wasn't. He was burning up.

She kept laughing, the giggles turning into something different, almost—she sagged a bit, pulling him off-balance with her. They slid to the floor, and then she was on his lap, and he was holding her while she sobbed. *Oh hell*. Nothing to make a guy feel helpless like a crying female. If it was any other woman, he probably would have gently patted her on the shoulder and made his excuses before hightailing it back to his man cave.

But he couldn't seem to help himself from wanting to take care of Lauren. *Oh, for Chrissakes. Get a loincloth and a vine to swing from, already.* He held her tighter and rocked a little bit and—God help him—kissed her hair.

After a few moments, she stopped crying, took a shuddering breath, and Mike loosened his arms a fraction, but not all the way. He wasn't quite ready to let her go. She turned her head away and wiped at her eyes with her shirtsleeves. "I'm so sorry." A sniffle. "I don't know what came over me."

Mike chuckled. "No? It's been such a quiet, serene couple of days."

She giggled.

"I think you get a free meltdown pass for this one." He knew he shouldn't, but he stroked her hair back from her forehead, turned her face toward him, then realized what he was doing. He dropped his hand so she could move off of his lap. If she wanted to. "You okay?"

She tilted her head at him and didn't move away. *Damn.* She was too close. Her lips were right there, soft and inviting, and her sweet body was pressed right up against the family mascot, who was standing at attention.

He felt her hands shift against his chest. It was an accident, he was sure it was, but her thumb brushed over his nipple and he jerked. He knew she realized where she'd touched him, because her eyes heated. She looked down at his mouth, then back into his eyes.

He was afraid to breathe. Then she licked her lips, and it was all over.

• • •

Mike's tongue was in her mouth, and his hands were on her butt, pressing her against him, and Lauren could feel...yes, that seemed to be an erection against her hip.

Oh God. Everything in her went full throb. His kiss trailed away from her mouth and over her jaw, down her neck. She had her hands in his hair and was about to shift so she could straddle him and get that hardness pressed where she needed it when she happened to look up and saw Chief Crawford standing a few feet away, leaning against the wall, smiling wide.

Mike must have felt her freeze, because he released the breast he had just cupped and cursed. Her boob was a little disappointed, too.

Crawford held up a hand. "Don't let me interrupt. I can wait."

"Crap." Lauren scrambled off of Mike's lap, hearing his *oof* as she rammed her hip somewhere he didn't need to be rammed, but she was too horrified to stop and apologize. She pushed her wet hair out of her face. Then she looked down and quickly crossed her arms over her chest. She was in a wet T-shirt and an unpadded bra. And it was cold in that hallway.

Mike got to his feet next to her and stood half a body width in front of Lauren, as though he would shield her from the cop, if need be. It would have been sweet if she wasn't so embarrassed.

"What do you need?" Mike asked, his voice low.

The cop pushed off the wall and approached, pulling his little notebook from his breast pocket. "I've got some more questions for the good doctor here." He stopped and gave Lauren a once over, then raised an eyebrow. "But maybe you want to get into something a little more comfortable?"

"Yeah, I can do that," Lauren said. She had a gym bag that she kept in the lab. It was probably the only thing that hadn't been touched by the vandals. She turned on her heel and went to grab the bag, then scurried down the hall to the ladies' room. Mike and Crawford spoke in low voices.

When the door shut behind her, she pulled off her wet jeans, leaving them inside out, and decided the panties needed to go, too. The heck with it, she could go commando in basketball shorts for an hour. Fortunately, she had a sports bra in her gym bag. She fought her way into that and topped off the whole ensemble with a T-shirt that advertised a scientific research supplier. It read, "Apoptosis: Cell Death Tour 2010" and had catalog numbers instead of concert tour dates on the back. It was nerd humor, but Lauren liked it. She wondered if Mike would, too.

Mike. *Whoa.* Looking into the mirror, she examined her puffy lips. She paused for a moment and touched her mouth, the feel of that kiss, those kisses, flooding through her again. She might have to rethink this "lust from afar" stance, because the real thing was definitely better than the fantasy.

She sighed. It didn't really matter. It wasn't like this was a real romance. She was a dull little science geek, and he was...Mike, the Freaking Hot as Hell Maintenance Man slash Knight in Shining Armor. He probably had some sort of damsel in distress fetish he was working out. This was just a...thing. A blip. A momentary indiscretion. Which was good. Because if it was real, she would forget to stand up for what she believed in and start letting Mike make the decisions about her life. He'd probably want to go back to being a cop in the big city, and she'd have to give up her position at Tucker, and even if she kept working, it wouldn't be as a full-time scientist. She'd find herself resentful and bitter, and he would start working more and more late hours, and...

Oh, dear Lord. He hadn't asked her to marry him. Or even for a date. It was just a blip. Although, she admitted to herself, she could use a little more blipping.

Finally dressed, she thought about stuffing her wet things back into her canvas gym bag but didn't want to soak her stash of Cosmos—treadmill reading material. Who said nerds didn't appreciate magazine crack? *Better use a plastic bag instead.* She wadded up the sodden mess and carried it back into the hall, cupping her hand underneath to catch the drips.

Mike and Crawford were standing close together in the hallway.

"Damn it, you are not going to drop this on my doorstep!" Mike's voice was low, barely audible, but he was clearly mad. He leaned toward the chief, jaw tight, shoulders tense, and his whole body appearing rather huge. She couldn't see Mike's eyes, but at her approach, the chief stepped back and raised his chin in her direction. She wasn't sure, but she thought she heard him mutter, "We'll get you someway."

Mike turned toward her, hand on his forehead, thumb on one side, fingers on the other, as though he were squeezing at a headache. He was soaked, T-shirt clinging to muscles, jeans to thighs. Calves. *Glutes.* "You got a mop in there?"

She nodded. "Culture room, behind the door."

He strode into the lab, leaving Lauren in the hallway with Crawford.

"Just a minute," she told Crawford, holding up her wet clothes." I've got to get a bag." He nodded and went back to propping up the corridor wall.

She went into the lab, too, but didn't follow Mike into the culture room. She wasn't sure what the rules were for near hookups in public places with a co-worker. Alex had been all dark rooms and closed doors, all the time. She transferred her wet clothes to her left hand and reached for a plastic trash bag with the other. Mike came out of the culture room and walked right up to her, backing her into the bench. She was so surprised that she dropped her wet clothes. Change spilled from the pocket of her jeans, coins pinging across the floor.

"Hey! You're getting me all wet again."

He grinned, and she realized what she'd just said. He leaned closer and put his mouth right to her ear. The tickle of his five o'clock shadow sent a shiver down her spine and…lower. "There's too much about this that is wrong time and wrong place." And then he dipped his chin a little more, brushing her skin with his lips.

She nodded. "Uh huh." But did he know why it was so wrong for her?

He backed up, holding her gaze for a moment before bending to pick up her wet clothes and putting them in the bag she held. He turned and bent down, reaching under the counter for some of the escaped coins while Lauren went for a quarter that had gone the other way. They both straightened at the same time. He gave her an odd look then, but didn't say anything, handing her the spilled change. She put it in the pocket of her shorts. It looked like he glanced at something in his hand before he stuck his fist in his own pocket.

She made a mental note: Ask Mike what he put in his pocket. But not now. Now she just needed to pretend like nothing had happened. Nothing. At. All.

Chapter Eleven

"Here, kitty, kitty," Mike said, tossing a wadded up ball of paper across the floor. Possum blinked at him from beneath the couch. "Come on, kitty. Time for your treat. Yum, yum!"

The cat closed her eyes and remained where she was.

The Devil's Ranger medallion that he'd picked up from the floor of Lauren's lab winked at him from the end table next to him. How did such a tiny bit of metal make his gut churn? If the spray painted tag on her tissue culture room wall wasn't a big enough neon sign, this was more evidence that Devil's Dust was surely coming from Lauren's lab.

And that it was almost as likely that Dylan was involved. There was no way that thing had gotten on the floor under the counter on its own.

The grandfather clock in the upstairs hallway chimed. Where the hell was Dylan?

To distract himself from the miserable confrontation to come, he considered calling Lauren to ask how to catch a reluctant cat for medicine-time. She was too smart to see that as anything other than what it was—a ploy to get her to come to his house. And once she was there…

Yeah, he wouldn't mind inviting her to stay for a beer or three, watch a few DVR'd episodes of *Justified*. And then he could kiss her again. And then…

The kitchen door creaked open.

"Perfect timing," Mike said. *Perfect to keep me from making a phone-pass at the scientist.* "Can you help me with this cat?"

Dylan came in and bent down in front of the couch. Possum immediately crawled out and wrapped herself around his ankles, purring. Dylan smirked at Mike and held out a hand.

Mike handed him the treat-wrapped pill and watched his brother expertly shove it into the cat's mouth, stroking her head while her motor ran as loud as a Harley. Mike stepped closer to try to get in a pet, but she hissed at him and raked her claws along his forearm.

"Shit!" He jerked his hand back. "Why does she hate me now? She liked me yesterday. Sort of. I buy the food. I clean the litter box. I'm the big dog."

Dylan didn't answer, just put the cat on the floor and picked up his backpack, heading toward the stairs. Possum retreated to her happy place under the couch.

"Hey, that was a pretty slick one you pulled on your boss today," Mike said, stopping Dylan in his tracks.

He turned and stared at Mike. "You following me around?"

"It looks like I need to."

Dylan's shoulders tensed, and he stared too steadily into

Mike's eyes. "I was doing her a favor."

"And if you'd gotten pulled over? How were you going to explain that you got her car impounded?"

"I didn't do anything to get pulled over for," Dylan shot back. "Damn, Mike. Give me a fucking break!"

Mike picked up the medallion and dangled it from the broken link. "I found this in her lab this afternoon. You want to explain *this*?"

Dylan didn't approach Mike to take the shiny silver charm. Instead, he held up both hands and backed away as though it were radioactive waste. "I don't know how that got there. I lost mine a long time ago."

"You apparently lost it at work."

"No, man. I lost it right after we moved here. I had it in my pocket, I was going to toss it into the lake, but when I got there, it was gone. I guess it fell out of a hole in my pocket or something." Dylan brushed the hair out of his eyes with a hand was shaking with nerves—or anger.

"That's convenient." He ran a hand through his own hair. "Dylan, if you're mixed up with these guys again, I can help. We'll figure something out. But you gotta stay away from Dino Romain."

"Why would you do this now? You didn't pay this much attention to me when I was actually trying to be a Ranger."

"Dylan—"

"You know what? Fuck this. You can believe me or not. I don't give a shit." He turned and went back the way he came in. Through the kitchen and out the back door.

"Dylan!" Mike went after him, but by the time he got to the back porch, Dylan was bumping over the curb on his bike. He disappeared into the twilight.

"Well, that went well," Mike said to Possum. She darted between his feet and disappeared up the stairs.

He picked up his phone and texted Dylan, but wasn't surprised when he didn't get an answer. He picked up his wallet and shoved it in his pocket, then plucked his truck keys from their hook by the door.

He knew he should probably let the kid cool off before confronting him again, but Mike had a bad feeling. Dylan had nearly gotten himself killed the last time he was mixed up with the Rangers. He might succeed this time, if Mike didn't find him and convince him to stay off the streets.

• • •

"Kevin, you have to accept that you're no longer a kitten," Lauren told her giant gray cat, shooing him off of the narrow windowsill next to her bed. The beast insisted on trying to sleep there every night—and every night, he fell off the ledge as soon as he dozed off. And he didn't land on his feet. Lauren figured the cat was on life 900 or so by now.

She pulled up her pink fleece sleep pants and dug around on the nightstand for a book to read. She wasn't really in the mood for a thriller, not after the real-life scary stuff that had happened over the last couple of days. She thought about the kisses she and Mike had shared that afternoon. Her lips still tingled. Nope, not reading a romance, either. She didn't need any more ideas than she already had.

Sad but true fact: Lauren was on her way to bed at nine on a Saturday.

The doorbell rang, and Kevin ran for the door. He was practically a Labrador retriever, the way he liked to investigate company. The bell rang again as she pulled on a robe and tied the sash. "Coming!" She looked through the peephole. *Holy schneikes.*

"Mike," she said, opening the door.

He glanced down at her, but his eyes were restless, darting to look inside her little house. "Is Dylan here?" he asked.

"What? No! Why on earth would he be here?"

"He's missing. We had…words, and he took off. I know he looks up to you, so I thought maybe…" He ran a hand through his hair, and it looked as though he'd done that several times already recently. "Shit. I'm sorry. I don't know what I was thinking by coming here."

She opened the door wider. "You'd better come in."

"No, I can see you're getting ready for bed." He looked at his watch, then over his shoulder, scanning the street.

"Yeah, well, that's because I have no life." She waved him in.

He entered, and her previously adequate living room shrank.

Kevin growled from between Lauren's feet. "Hang on. Let me toss this guy." She picked Kevin up and moved around Mike to the door. Kevin departed with a hiss and a glare.

"Do I smell like a dog or something?"

"Huh?" Lauren leaned toward him and sniffed. No, he smelled like Bounce and sexy man—something she wanted to roll around and wrap herself in. "No…no dog smell that I can tell."

"I can almost understand why your cat wouldn't like me, you just threw him out and let me in. But mine doesn't like me, either. I'm developing a complex."

"Maybe you're just all 'King of the Jungle,' and they see you as competition." Lauren realized that sounded a little too flirty and quickly said, "Do you want something to drink?"

"You got a Diet Coke?"

That gave her a moment's pause. She'd have taken Mike to be a beer kind of a guy. Or regular Coke, at any rate. "No, sorry. I've got grape Kool-Aid, though."

"Water's fine." He followed her into the tiny kitchen. "Just show me where the glasses are."

She pointed at the dish drainer, watched him fill the vintage Marvin the Martian glass and then drink it down before refilling. His big hand dwarfed the glass, Marvin peering from between his fingers. "What about Evan? Did you check with him?"

"Yeah, I did. And, no, he didn't go there."

"You want to tell me what happened?"

Mike put the glass on the counter, then dug something out of his pocket. "Do you recognize this?" He handed her a medallion of some sort, about an inch and a half in diameter, made of silvery metal. It had a weird dent a little off-center, like it had been bashed with a blunt object.

"No," she said, then turned it over in her palm. There was a design on the other side, distorted by the convex surface, but it looked like… "Does this match the graffiti in my lab?"

"It's not yours?"

"No, why would you think that?"

"I don't, but I found it on the floor next to the change that fell out of your pocket after…"

She looked up and found him looking at her, but she

couldn't read his expression. "You can say it. After I attacked you in the hall."

"After we kissed. Yes." He held her gaze, one side of those gorgeous lips quirked up. There was definitely heat there, she thought. Definitely maybe. Why had she sworn off relationships again? Or at least…blipping?

Lauren cleared her throat, suddenly wanting to take a drink of water from Mike's glass. So to speak. Instead, she looked back down at the medallion. So that's what he'd slipped into his pocket back at the lab. Like Bilbo. Definitely not Gollum, because that dude never wore clothes. "Um. So, I've never seen it before. Why didn't you ask me about it then?" Instead, he'd mopped up the water in the hallway and disappeared while she'd talked to Chief Crawford.

Mike shook his head. "I had to talk to Dylan first. Give him a chance to come clean."

Lauren sank onto a kitchen chair. "And did he? Come clean?" She prayed Dylan hadn't confessed—because she also prayed that he wasn't guilty. Not just for Dylan's sake, but for Mike's, too.

Dylan was such a nice kid. But she was easy to fool. She knew that.

Mike pulled out the other chair and sat, leaning toward Lauren. Knees spread, he draped his arms over his thighs, hands dangling. "Nope."

"So what happened? You accused him and he blew up?"

"Something like that. I asked about his medallion from when he was a Ranger. He claimed he hadn't kept it, but I don't believe him. He reminded me…"

"What?"

He took a breath and let it out. "That I hadn't bothered

to look out for him before, so why start now?"

At the bleak look on this big, strong man's face, Lauren reached out and took the hand holding the medallion in both of hers. "I don't believe he did it," she told him despite the sprouting stem of a tiny seed of doubt. "I just—there was nothing in his demeanor today that said guilty. He came into the lab and dove into helping clean up and talked about internet things—of which I have no understanding—just like always."

Mike pulled his hand away and stared through the back door window. "I wish I could be as sure as you are. But he's lied before." He turned back to face her.

They were quiet for a moment, just looking at each other. She bit her bottom lip, catching herself in the middle of the unconscious move. His eyes dipped to her mouth, then lower. He smiled slightly. She realized her robe had come undone, and the thin T-shirt she wore did little to disguise the fact that she was braless. Something Mike seemed to be quite aware of as he continued to stare and his eyes got a little glossy. Wow. Her breasts had hypnotized someone? Someone totally hot. Mike. She wondered if she could use this power for naughtiness...

Her breath caught and her heartbeat accelerated before she forced herself to remember that she wasn't going to get involved with him. Although, involved might be a bit ambitious. She would guess that he didn't do relationships. Which was good. Because neither did she.

His phone rang then, breaking the spell, thank goodness.

"Evan," he said, after accepting the call. "No, I haven't found him yet." He frowned as he listened.

Lauren figured she should give him some privacy as he

spoke with his brother and headed to her room to check emails on her own phone. She glanced at the senders but saw nothing of importance—just one from Mrs. Althea Guanadonamaribo, probably claiming that she'd won the Canadian lottery, but was stranded in Zimbabwe, and all Lauren needed to do was send a check for $1,000 to get a cut of the haul. She scrolled further and saw an email from the Pemberton people—number forty-three of the eighty-nine she'd be receiving to remind her of her appointment. Right…like she could forget that.

She sat down on the edge of the bed and plugged the phone into the charger just as another email pinged her screen. She opened that one. Her mother, sending a picture of that cat with the grumpy face that said, "Still here… Worst apocalypse ever."

Only Lauren's mother would think that it was appropriate to send an end of the world joke when her world—or at least, her career—might very well be ending. And only Lauren would think it was the funniest thing she'd seen all day. She reminded herself to call her mom in the morning. No one could make lemonade out of life's curve balls like Karen Kane.

Lauren arrived back in the kitchen just as Mike said, "Sure, I'll call you if I hear anything."

After Mike snapped the phone shut and shoved it into his pocket, he cursed. His concern seemed a little out of proportion to the situation.

"I know you're worried," she said. "But Dylan *is* an adult. Does he have a girlfriend?"

"Maybe, but I don't think so. Not since Angela, the sister of the leader of the Rangers. But he ended that when he got in trouble."

Lauren remembered something from earlier in the day, which watered the doubt sprout taking root in her brain. "When he left to deliver the pig, he called someone—a friend—he said he was going to have ride along with him. Do you know who that could be?"

Mike shook his head. "He's pretty much a loner, as far as I can tell. He does some online gaming stuff, and I'm sure has some virtual friends out there somewhere, but honestly, except to come to school and go to the library, he almost never leaves the house." He pushed away from the counter. "I should take off. I need to look for him."

"Where will you go?"

He stopped, turning back to her. "I have no idea."

"Look. He's over eighteen. Maybe not far enough over to make good choices, but they're his choices. There's no point in driving yourself crazy."

"You sound like my grandmother."

"I'm going to pretend like you didn't compare me to your grandmother. Although I'm sure she was a lovely person."

He smiled again. "You know what I mean."

"Yeah, I do. And you're right. I assume you've left him messages?"

He nodded.

She took a deep breath, then leaped off the cliff. "Okay, then why don't you sit down and chill for a while. Maybe he'll check in. Give it an hour. If he doesn't call, I'll go out looking for him with you. We'll go to the Emergency Room and call the police."

"I already did that. The ER and police."

"Then we'll do it again. Come on. I've got a boxed set of

Dr. Who that I haven't seen."

"Are you a big fan of *Dr. Who*?"

"Not really."

He heaved a sigh of relief.

She laughed. "Maybe we can find a movie on cable."

"Can it have bombs and car chases?"

"Only if it's also got The Rock or Jason Statham without a shirt."

He laughed, too, and followed her into the living room.

• • •

Mike tried to watch the movie. But his attention was divided between worrying about Dylan and smelling Lauren's sweet fragrance, being warmed by her heat across the whole couch cushion between them, feeling her shift every now and then.

Lauren didn't seem too concerned about Dylan's possible involvement in the vandalism and said that his work ethic and attention to detail were enough evidence that he was honest. That was a bit of a stretch for Mike, but he and Lauren came from two different worlds, where trust was concerned. She had a weird openhearted thing going on that Mike didn't think could be faked. He hadn't known many people who were that...nice.

Here they were, sitting on the couch, watching a movie like they'd been dating long enough to stay in instead of going out. Like it was a date in the first place. That was a concept that didn't disturb Mike as much as he might have preferred until he imagined her relying on him, trusting him to be there to do the right thing.

A couple of times, Lauren got up and went into the

kitchen, opened the back door, and called out for the cat she'd let outside.

"Does he take off very often?"

"No, he's usually only gone for an hour or so at a time, then he jumps up and hangs onto the door molding until I open it."

"Well, maybe he's got a girlfriend somewhere and he's shacking up."

"Yeah, maybe."

Mike dug his phone out of his pocket and checked the screen for the fiftieth time. Nothing.

"If Dylan's ignoring your calls," she said, getting up and wiping buttery fingers on a paper napkin, "he might answer mine."

"Worth a try."

He watched her walk down the hall toward where he assumed was her bedroom. Her curves weren't obvious, but she made the fuzzy bathrobe look mighty appealing. *Damn.* Maybe he should go before he made a move on her and forgot that he needed to find his brother .

"Hey!" she called from the end of the hall, reappearing with her phone held high in triumph. "Guess who's been texting me?"

"No shit?" Mike stood up and met her in the middle of the living room. "What did he say?"

"There are a bunch of texts here, and I don't think they came in order." She pushed some buttons and read for a minute, then laughed and handed Mike the phone.

He took it from her, felt the brush of her hand during the exchange. She held onto his forearm and stood on tiptoe to look at the screen with him. He transferred the phone to his left hand and put his right arm around her shoulders so she could see.

They both froze. She looked up at him, startled at his proximity. He started to remove his arm, but then she leaned into him and looked back at the phone.

cant deal wth hs blsht rt now

Just tkn wlk clr my head

See mikes @ ur house. tell him im ok if hes lookn 4 me

Mike typed back and hit send. *Glad you're ok. Call Evan.* "I should make sure he goes home."

"No, you shouldn't," she said. "He's a big boy."

She was probably right. But any time he'd left Dylan to his own devices, bad things happened. Was this a time when he needed to let go? Or was he rationalizing, because he just wanted to wrap himself around Lauren and explore her soft sweet skin until—

Lauren's phone buzzed again.

Chapter Twelve

If Mikes at ur hse NOT looking 4 me, tell him I won't wait up.

Lauren had never felt more like a nerd than she did in that moment, because she was only sort of sure she knew what Dylan was implying. And she didn't need a mirror to know she was blushing. She could feel every capillary in her body dilating. Every nerve felt alive. So it was probably embarrassment that made Mike's breath feel like a caress along her neck. There were probably some pheromone receptors in her skin that were flirting with his manly-man essences. Her vision was a little hazy, and her brain had definitely shut down, but the rest of her was alive and kicking.

She felt the weight of his arm around her shoulders, his warmth and strength.

"Sorry," Mike said, low and soft, the vibration of his chuckle sending a thrill down her back. "He shouldn't have said that."

Lauren opened her mouth to reply, but she stopped

when she felt a brush of heat against the base of her skull. He had moved a little behind her, his arm circled around her waist. His open mouth barely moved over the skin of her neck, right where it met her shoulder.

He pulled the phone from her hand, pushing the button that made the screen go dark, and she felt him drop it into the pocket of her robe.

"I did come here looking for Dylan," he said. "But I'm not looking for him now."

One big hand spread across her stomach, pressing her back against his front. She let her head fall back onto his shoulder, and his other hand came up to cradle her jaw, holding her head still for the caress of his lips along her collarbone. His breath quavered a bit, which made Lauren's back arch, which in turn pressed her backside against his groin. He wanted her. She was suddenly—distinctly—less nerdy. Nerds avoided involvement with take-charge, alpha men. Nerds didn't...*blip* with hot maintenance men. She was, she decided, definitely about to *blip*.

"I'll go if you think I should, but I'd like it if you let me stay." Teeth scraped along the tendon at the side of her neck. "Just for a little while."

"Uh-huh," was all she could get out.

The hand on her jaw moved lower, parting the lapels of her robe to slide over her body to cup her breast. She covered his hand with hers, guiding him to press against a nipple that ached for more. Her mouth was open, she needed to do something with it, but what...? Kissing. Kissing would be good. She turned and wrapped her arms around his neck and pulled his mouth to hers. She was starving, and he was... tasty.

Her body was swollen and achy, and she pressed against him for relief, but it wasn't enough. He put his big hands on her backside and pulled her against his pelvis. She was tall enough that the apex of her mound met the base of his erection, and she stood on her tiptoes, trying to get higher, to get more contact between them. He lifted one of her legs and pulled her even closer to where she needed to be.

The phone in her pocket chimed with an incoming text, causing them both to jump. Mike loosened his hold on her leg, and she stood on both of her feet again, breathing heavily. They stared at each other for an instant, then Lauren reached into her pocket and pulled out her phone.

Another text from Dylan.

Close ur shades.

"Ack!" Lauren stepped back from Mike, looking frantically toward the front window, which indeed bore neither shade nor curtain.

"Jesus Christ," Mike muttered, striding to the window. He peered into the darkness outside, but Lauren knew he couldn't see anything, because her reflection, disheveled, panting, took up the whole window. He pulled the cord that closed the drapes.

The phone chimed again.

Going home now. ;-)

Mike came back to where Lauren stood, searching her eyes, letting her see how much he wanted her, but giving her room to back away. And maybe that's why she was standing right there, with him, in this moment. As she stared back at him, she realized they were both in a weird place in their lives, both careers hanging because of some messed up drug dealer's whim.

She reached a hand to his face, feeling his hard jaw beneath faint stubble heating her palm. He didn't move, but his eyelids lowered the tiniest fraction over pupils that expanded.

Their paths would probably diverge soon enough, but for right now...right now they were in the same place, literally and figuratively, and Lauren, for one, wanted to stay a little longer.

There were reasons she shouldn't take this any further, she knew there were. She shoved them into a mental shoebox and crammed it out of sight.

"This way," she said, taking Mike's hand. He let her pull him down the hall.

Entering the bedroom, she saw that the shades were closed, but then pulled the drapes over them for good measure while Mike shut the door and turned the lock. "I live here alone," she told him.

"I don't care. I don't trust your cat not to let himself back in the house, and the only claws I want to feel on my ass are yours."

She huffed out a laugh when he pulled her back into his arms and kissed her again.

They tumbled to the bed. Mike growled and pushed half a dozen throw pillows onto the floor. He pushed her onto her back as he leaned over her and opened her robe. They both watched him caress her breasts through the thin T-shirt she wore. He didn't focus on her nipples, and instead pressed and molded her breasts, squeezing and making her gasp.

He shot a quick glance at her face and must have recognized that the sound was from pleasure, not pain, because he repeated the move, dipping his head to finally take one nipple into his mouth, fabric and all. He sucked hard, then bit gently. Lauren writhed against him, until the need to touch her bare skin to his bare skin had her pulling away and shrugging out of her robe.

He pulled his shirt over his head and threw it across the room. Lauren had a glimpse of a chest and belly that should be on the cover of a men's health magazine. There were a couple of white scars running through the hair that covered his pecs before arrowing toward his navel and down into his jeans. He reached for her, grabbed the hem of her shirt, and pulled it over her head, but halted there, trapping her arms in the fabric. He pressed her back into the mattress, holding her wrists above her head. He dropped his full weight on top of her and kissed her again, tongue and lips sliding and sucking and nipping. His chest hair felt soft against her swollen, aching nipples.

She parted her legs to feel his erection rock against her again and again through his denim and her pajama pants. It was almost perfect, almost…right there. Tension fought with surrender, and without warning, currents of feeling swamped her, and oh, God, she was coming, right there, right then. Waves of heat spread from her core through her spine and legs and arms. She heard herself cry out while every muscle in her body tightened to hold on to the feeling.

When the orgasm eased, her arousal was only higher, and she wanted—*needed*—to feel him inside her. She took one of his hands and slid it between them. He rose slightly to his knees to let her get to his belt, but she was fumble-fingered.

He rolled onto his back to get to the buckle, and she followed, straddling his thighs. She ran her hands along his thick arms, and he laughed, looking away from his belt to kiss her. "You're not helping."

"Sorry. I just need…I want to touch you."

"Yeah, I'm on board with that."

Finally his buckle was undone, and it was her turn to push him back onto the mattress, slipping her fingers inside the waistband of his jeans to work at the button there. The soft hair on his stomach stroked the backs of her fingers, and she bent to kiss him just above his belly button. He sucked in a breath.

She pulled the tab of his zipper, careful with the smooth head of his penis and the hard length below. She stopped to spread a drop of pre-ejaculate and sighed when he twitched under her hand. She'd never thought penises were particularly attractive, but this one should be in a textbook of extraordinary anatomy.

She looked up at him, saw he was watching her face, felt him twitch again when their eyes met. "You always go commando?" she had to ask.

"Uh…" His hands stroked her thighs and she wished her pajama pants would magically disappear. "I'll plead the Fifth. Oh, God, do that again."

"What?" She looked down, saw that she had her hand wrapped around him and was holding on for dear life.

"Squeeze me like that. Yeah." His head arched back as he thrust into her hand. How could he be so powerful and vulnerable at the same time?

"I need…" She started to push her pants down her hips.

He began to do the same, but then he froze when he got his pants to mid-thigh. "Oh, no."

"What?"

"I don't suppose you have..." His jaw was tight, eyes wary.

"You don't have a condom in your wallet?"

He shook his head.

"I thought that was like, a guy rule."

He laughed ruefully and sat up, propping his elbows on his knees, jeans hindering his movements. "I ah, wasn't planning on this. And I don't usually have spontaneous sex..."

That made her feel good. He had passion...but it didn't make him crazy.

"Ah, hell," he said, starting to lean back and pull his pants up.

"Maybe we could—" She ran her hand over his hard stomach, down...

He interrupted her quest with a hand over hers. "It's no big deal."

"It looks pretty big to me."

He snort-laughed but must have seen her consternation, because he stopped fighting his zipper. Pulling her into his arms, he flopped back onto the mattress with a groan, her head on his chest. He tucked her head back against him, buried his fingers in her hair. She was gratified that his hand was a little unsteady. "What I mean is, you're not obligated to get me off, just because—"

"Yeah, I know, I'm not *obligated*," she said, letting a shred of peevishness slip out.

"That didn't come out right. Uh, it may be a few minutes before the blood starts flowing back to my brain. Maybe we can just lay here for a minute and let the blue fade—"

She laughed. Okay, that helped. At first she was afraid that he was okay with calling a halt to things because he wasn't too enthusiastic about *things* in the first place. Which was totally insecurity talking.

She listened to his heartbeat under her ear for a few seconds, then muttered, "But I do want to reciprocate."

"Oh, darlin', there isn't too much I'd like more than that."

But the moment had passed, she recognized that. For now.

She smiled, and he smiled right back at her, sending a thrill through her that somehow got stuck in the center of her chest.

• • •

Mike ran his hand down Lauren's smooth back and then up to bury it in her hair, which was a golden mess. Her eyes flickered in the lamplight, and he lost himself in the caramel brown color…was that hazel? No, hazel was blue and green, or blue and—who the fuck cared?

He'd given her beard burn—her cheeks and breasts were red. He felt absurdly proud of that, as though he'd marked his territory. Although, maybe giving her his class ring or letting her wear his letterman jacket—if he'd gotten one back in the day—would have been gentler on her silky skin.

She was quiet, still snuggled up to him, but a little stiff, clearly thinking about something.

"I should probably go?" His statement came out more of a question.

She sat up, pulling the sheet up to cover her still naked

breasts. "Are you asking me if I want you to go? 'Cause I don't want you to leave… I mean, you don't have to stay… or whatever. I'm not like, you know, going to expect you to move in and ask me to marry you—I mean, I'm not gonna go all *Fatal Attraction* here, but you don't have to rush off…" She sat up. "Oh, hell. I'm overthinking this, aren't I? I don't normally do this sort of thing, as trite as it sounds, and I don't really know what the protocol is. I rarely even date, much less make out with guys I barely know."

"What about old what's his name? Mister Pink Shirt, back at your lab on the first day we met?"

"Alex?" She rolled her eyes. "Oh, there was protocol there. There was everything but a Yahoo calendar and a contract. Which is probably why we worked together for three years and were…involved…for about fifteen minutes."

As she spoke, he bent to untie the laces of his boots. He straightened and kicked them off, and then lay down next to her, but on top of the covers, facing her on his side. She lay back down, too. Her lips were swollen from his kisses, and he wanted to kiss her again. "I might stick around for a few more minutes," he said. "My legs seem to be a little rubbery still."

"Oh." She blushed.

He had to reach out and push her hair behind her ear. "I don't know if there's a protocol here, either. It can be whatever you want it to be."

"Apropos of nothing but post-intimacy pillow talk, what's with you and Evan?" she asked.

"I don't know," Mike hedged. He wasn't ready to take all the family skeletons for a walk in the light just yet. The thing with him and Evan…

"It's complicated," she concluded for him. "Okay."

He shrugged. He wasn't comfortable sharing his secrets. So why did he feel like opening up to her?

"Evan can be a little hard to take sometimes."

"That's a lot of it," Mike agreed. At least, that was a lot of it now. It wasn't where it had started, but he wasn't going there. "I mean, I know he's smarter than me. He's got the diplomas to prove it, so maybe he's earned that attitude."

"He doesn't have more diplomas than I do."

"Your college probably didn't give out the one for snobby brainiacs. Not that you would have been awarded that. Um, not the snotty part, at any rate. The brainiac part, though." He couldn't resist leaning over to kiss her. He appreciated that she didn't talk down to him or downplay her own brainpower. Smart was very sexy.

"Ha! Snotty Braniac 101 is the only thing I flunked, besides gym. Besides, there's a lot more to 'smart' than numbers and letters." Her voice was getting lower, sleepy. She snuggled closer to him and curled her hand against his chest. The next sound she made was a soft snore.

Mike reached behind him and turned off the lamp on the nightstand. He had to get back on the track of Devil's Dust, but he couldn't do anything about it tonight. Not with a glorious, albeit sleeping woman in his arms. In the morning, he'd swallow his pride and check in with Crawford.

Lauren made a cute little snuffle and smiled in her sleep. His breath went a little shallow all of a sudden. He couldn't get in too deep with her. He wanted to think that it was because he didn't want to lead her on, didn't want to break her heart, but thought that maybe the opposite was more likely to be true.

But he was here tonight. In her bed. It wasn't like he could un-ring her doorbell. Too bad there hadn't been any condoms…

He lay there a little while longer, feeling her warm, soft body curled up against him. After a few minutes, he kissed her on the forehead, then slipped off of the bed and picked up his boots and shirt. He had an errand to run. And it wasn't one that could wait until morning.

Chapter Thirteen

The theme song from *The Big Bang Theory* rent Lauren's slumber, and she jumped from sexy dreams to blind-groping for her phone, hoping to quiet it before it woke Mike.

She didn't look at the display before she hit the answer button, so she was surprised to hear Alex say, "Hello? Lauren?"

"Um...hang on," she whispered, then turned to see that she was alone in her bed.

Crap. Mike was gone. He'd snuck out. She must have misunderstood him. Maybe he hadn't really wanted to stay with her, and he was trying to be nice until he could escape. She had no idea how these things worked. With Alex, there had been so much negotiating and boundary setting before they slept together, she was amazed they'd managed to actually get tab A aligned with slot B. With Mike...tab A hadn't even gotten close to slot B yet, and...yowza. Oh, well. It was supposed to be just a blip. Ions passing in solution. Not an exothermic reaction of nuclear proportions.

"Lauren? You okay?"

"Yeah. Sorry, Alex." She touched Mike's side of the bed. It was still warm. She shook off her disappointment and focused on the call. "What time is it? What's wrong?"

"It's midnight. I know it's late, but I just heard about what happened to your lab and I wanted to make sure you're okay."

Lauren did a double take before she moved the phone from her ear and checked the caller ID. Yep. This person who sounded like Alex was calling from Alex's number. The Alex she'd been involved with would never have called to check on her. He would have waited until it was convenient, and then delivered a lecture on what she could have done differently to avoid her problems. "I'm okay. A little freaked out, a lot mad, but okay."

"Are you sure? What happened? What was taken?"

Lauren gave Alex a brief rundown of the damage. "And they took that ancient desktop computer and some notebooks."

"So did they take any of your drug?"

"Um…" How much should she tell him? What did it matter? "They took the step two. And a bag of step one pellets."

Alex whistled. "Uh-oh. That's bad."

"I don't see how. They can't know what to do with it. They don't have my notes."

"I thought you said they took your notebooks."

"Oh. Yeah. But they didn't get the right ones."

"Thank God. Do you have them somewhere safe?"

"Yeah, I think so." She hesitated, because he would

probably gloat about having convinced her to do things his way. "I brought them home to transcribe onto my laptop."

"That's a good idea. I'm glad you took my advice."

Of course he was. She needed to get him off of the phone before he took every detail and dissected it until she found herself defending not only her own choices, but the logic of the vandals and the parents who mistreated them into taking up a life of crime.

"You know, Alex, I'm really not up for talking about this right now. I appreciate your concern, but…"

"Of course. It's late, and I'm sure you've got better things to do right now." This was said with a tone that Lauren couldn't quite interpret.

"Yeah," she said, mentally searching for an excuse to get off the phone. "I've got to find my cat."

They said goodbye, then she hung up. God, why did she let Alex push all the wrong buttons? Probably because when they'd been together, he'd rarely pushed any of the right ones.

Funny how she hadn't noticed how wrong he'd been for her until she met Mike. What had it been…two days? Three? Except…was Mike better for her, or worse? Her body was definitely on the "keep him around" side, but her brain—and her knowledge of how life worked—said he was just as bad, if not worse, than Alex. Alex had tried to micromanage her life. But Mike? If she wasn't careful, she'd be begging Mike to take *everything* she was and everything she had, even if he didn't want it.

And he probably didn't. He'd sneaked out of her bed in the dark of night like this had been some kind of a phantom booty call or something. She shouldn't judge him for disappearing. It was kind of surprising that he'd hung out with her. Sitting around on the couch watching movies couldn't be the most exciting way he'd imagined spending his Saturday night, even if he was distracted with worry over Dylan. And then she'd attacked him, and then when he didn't have a condom, practically begged him to let her give him a hand job. How pathetic was that?

Just as well that he'd left. She was already thinking about how his boots would look propped up on her coffee table every night. How his laundry would fit so nicely in the hamper next to hers. Something achy and painful bumped around just under her breastbone.

This was better, though. No awkward morning after stuff.

Pulling on her pajama pants, she went to the door to let Kevin in. Except he wasn't sitting on the stoop, waiting for her. She stuck her head out and called to him, shaking a box of kitty treats, but he still didn't come. This wasn't Kevin's MO. The cat always came back at night. Tension flashed up her spine. Time to go look for the purr-bucket.

She shoved her feet into sneakers without socks. Grabbing the flashlight and her cell phone, she let herself out and locked the door behind her.

Walking down the driveway to the sidewalk, she noticed a dark pickup truck parked in front of her next door neighbor's house. It kind of looked like Mike's. Oh great. Now she was going to think every dark truck she saw was Mike. She'd probably start looking for him at the grocery store, too. She rubbed that spot on her sternum.

She vowed to herself and the stars that if she ever found herself driving past his house, she'd check herself into rehab somewhere.

A small, black Honda with shiny silver spinner rims and a broken taillight sat idling a little farther down the street. College kids lived in several houses on her street, and they had company coming and going at all times of day and night.

She strolled along, shining her flashlight at the neighbor's bushes, calling, "Here, kitty! Come on out, Kevin!" but there was no answering "meow."

As she came upon the little black car, she glanced through the windshield and then looked away, realizing that the couple inside was in a serious clinch. But before she reached the tail end, she pulled up short. There was something painted on the rear fender. That symbol—the same that had been spray painted on her lab wall and embossed on the medallion Mike had showed her. It was the Devil's Ranger's gang sign.

Oh, shit. She involuntarily looked back at the interior of the car, and the couple inside was staring at her. The guy, whose face was already in shadow, quickly turned his head and slumped down, but the girl stared right at her.

Lauren felt like a rabbit, paralyzed with fear. Okay. She could play the concerned neighbor. Besides, she was holding the world's heaviest flashlight. If all else failed, she could throw it at them and run. She smiled into the car. The guy seemed to be saying something to the girl, who waved him off and rolled down the window.

The young woman, pretty, with long dark hair and too much eyeliner, leaned over the center console, across the guy's lap, and returned Lauren's smile.

"Are we doing something wrong?" she asked.

"Um…" Lauren thought fast. "I just wanted to ask if you've seen a cat. My cat. It's missing."

The guy didn't look up at her, which was a little creepy. But if he was her drug thief, maybe he was someone she might recognize from campus. She was relieved to see that his hands were visible, one on the girl's shoulder, the other elbow on the door of the open window. At least he wasn't holding a gun on her.

"Nooo…" The girl looked at her like she was crazy, and Lauren supposed she was. What was she doing?

"Hey! What the fuck is going on here?" The low male voice came from behind.

Lauren straightened and bumped her head on something hard. "Ow!" she said.

Turning, she saw Mike rubbing his chin, glaring at her from beneath lowered brows.

After her heart landed back in her chest, she recognized both relief and annoyance—extreme annoyance—at Mike. "What the hell? What's up with you sneaking up on me?"

He didn't answer, instead moved past her to approach the car, which revved and squealed away from the curb.

And as much as the scientist in her recognized the fact that it was probably a *good* thing the car with a gang symbol had left her neighborhood, the other part of her was simply pissed that Mike had chased off what could have been a lead to her getting back her drug.

• • •

As soon as Mike knew Lauren was safe, his protective instincts were channeled directly into anger. Apparently, that's where her fear went, too, because suddenly, she was right up in his face.

"What the hell are you doing?" she demanded. "Those were *suspects*! I'll never find them again!"

"Are you out of your fucking mind?" he barked. He knew he was being a dick, but damn! What was she doing out here talking to someone in a Ranger's car? "You look like you're making a drug deal out here in the middle of the night!"

"What? Are you accusing me of"—she waved her hands around—"being a...a...bad guy? In my *jammies*?"

He almost laughed then, but he was still too pissed off. "No. I'm just saying that car—that was a Devil's Ranger tag on the bumper. What the hell are you doing out here, anyway?"

"Looking for my stupid cat!" She crossed her arms, tucking that ridiculous flashlight against her body.

Oh. When he'd come around the corner and seen her leaning into the car—for just an instant—he'd thought he was about to interrupt a drug deal. That was just how he was conditioned. When he saw someone on a dark street, leaning to talk to someone in a car, in his experience, that meant there was some sort of an illegal transaction about to take place.

But then he nearly panicked when he realized that it was *his* woman who was standing on the street in silver Converse low tops and pink pajama pants covered with singing frogs, holding a flashlight. Drug dealers might wear their pajamas and stupid shoes outside at night, but they didn't carry flashlights.

Wait... *His* woman? When had he started thinking that way?

"No, I don't think that you're a bad guy," he finally said.

"No? Are you sure? Maybe I trashed my own lab. Maybe I stole my own drug and then set it up so it would be impossible for me to make more any time soon. Maybe I let a former cop into my house so that I could, what, pretend to be honest? Or distract you with sexual favors so my other posse peeps could do nefarious posse things?"

"You're not a bad guy." He was definitely trying not to laugh now, because he wasn't sure if she was still mad.

She narrowed her eyes, making an exaggerated scowl. "How can you be so sure?"

"You're carrying a flashlight. Bad guys don't carry flashlights unless they're dragging a body through the woods to a shallow grave."

"How do you know? Is it in the bad guy handbook?" Lauren crossed her arms and pinched her mouth before apparently giving up and letting a smile work its way across her face.

He stood there like an idiot for a few seconds, just looking at her, before he remembered what had started their micro-tiff. "So what did they say to you? Who was in the car?"

"A pretty girl and her boyfriend. We didn't get to the Facebook friend stage before you showed up and scared them off."

"I wonder what they were doing out here."

"Making out."

Which reminded him of what he and Lauren had been doing less than an hour ago.

She looked at the bag he carried. "What's that? Where did you go?"

"Uh…" He shoved the bag behind his back. "I just went for a walk."

"Did you go meet *your* drug dealer?" She was smiling.

Something loosened in Mike's chest. He hadn't realized it had gotten tight. "No…"

"What is it?" She tried to reach around him to grab the bag, but he was taller than her, so he held it above his head. "Come on, show me." She had to lean against him on her tiptoes to try to get it, but she still couldn't reach.

He liked the way that felt. "Um, I don't want you to think I'm making assumptions." He lowered his arm and handed her the bag.

She opened it and looked inside, then handed it back to him. Turning to walk away, she shot back over her shoulder. "Interesting. I'm going back home to bed. Alone. But you hang on to that. You might need it sometime."

Mike stood on the sidewalk and watched until she unlocked the door. She went inside, turned off the porch light, and latched the door.

He unlocked his truck and tossed the bag containing a box of condoms on the seat beside him. Sure, they hadn't put them to use, but as he started the truck to head home, he realized he was oddly feeling happier than he had in a long time.

• • •

Lauren locked the front door and turned off the porch light before peering out of the window. Mike had been smiling as he got in his truck. He'd sat for a minute staring at her house, then shook his head and drove off.

She sighed, doing a little happy dance on her way down the hall. He hadn't bailed out on her, after all. No, the man had gone off and bought condoms. What did it say that she found a guy making a midnight trip to the condom store the most romantic thing she'd experienced in...ever?

She took off her shoes, put the flashlight and her phone on the nightstand, and crawled between the sheets. She grabbed the pillow that Mike had used for such a short time. It smelled like him. If she was a total dork, she'd put it in a plastic bag to preserve that smell, only getting it out when she needed a fix.

She knew someone who studied volatile aromatics. She could get her to put the pillowcase through her magic sensor machine and break it down to its elemental ingredients and recreate it. She'd probably have to find a way to biopsy Mike to get some sweat gland cells to clone...

Okay, maybe she was drifting into science fiction with that fantasy, but it kept her smiling while she hugged the pillow to her chest and curled up around it.

Chapter Fourteen

Lauren peered into the misty dawn. "Kevin! Here, kitty, kitty!"

Nothing.

She shivered, a reaction that had nothing to do with the cool morning and everything to do with concern over her cat. He'd never, *ever* stayed out all night. He didn't go in for the whole caterwauling thing. If he wasn't back by suppertime, she'd start making posters to hang around campus. She told herself that he'd probably been invited into the home of some students who were feeding him sushi and letting him on the kitchen table.

Shutting the front door, she picked up her tea and cell phone and settled in at the kitchen table. She needed to let her mother know that she was still alive—especially after her little dramatic melt down on Thursday. And maybe for some girl talk.

Her mother answered on the first ring. "What's wrong?"

"Why do you think something's wrong?" Just because she'd woken up this morning with visions of long walks on a beach holding hands with a certain guy didn't make anything wrong, did it?

"Well, you did have that little vandalism issue at work the other day, right?"

"True," Lauren agreed. "But no, there's been no more trouble in the lab."

"Then what?"

Okay, yeah. There was something wrong. And she might as well talk about it, since this was why she'd called. "I kind of met someone."

"And you have a problem with having met someone? A man? Or a woman? Where did you meet him—her?"

"No. Mom. It's—he's a guy. From work. But—"

"Is he married?"

"No, he's single, but—"

"He's not another scientist, is he?"

"Why would it be bad if it was another scientist?"

"It wouldn't be bad. The Professor's a scientist!"

"I know. And because Dad was a scientist, you had to quit being one to be my mom."

Her mom laughed. "Oh, honey. I didn't have to quit work to be your mom. I *got* to quit. I hated every minute of being in that lab. I loved the *idea* of being a scientist, but I sucked at it. The reality of being a stay-at-home mom was way better."

Lauren was speechless. "You're kidding."

"No. I thought you knew that."

The world tilted a little and got a little fuzzy. "But then when I was going out with Alex, why did you tell me he would ruin my dream to be a scientist?"

"Because he's a...a big jerk. He was always telling you what to do and how to do it."

Things were suddenly much clearer. Why was it that she'd taken so many years to understand what her mother had done with her life? Why hadn't she acted like a scientist and asked her mom rationally why she'd given up on being a scientist, instead staying in the preconceived Land of Assumptions? "Oh."

There was silence on the line for a moment while Lauren digested the conversation.

"Lauren? Are you okay?"

"Um, yeah. I think so."

"So who is this guy? What's he like?"

Rock and roll and fast cars. Thunder and lightning. Soft kisses and sweaty sex. "He...he's definitely not a scientist."

Her mother laughed. "Good. You need someone who will help you remember there's more to life than notebooks and formulas."

"Yeah...maybe." *At least until he notices that I'm really boring.*

"And when are we going to meet him?"

"Don't set an extra plate for Christmas dinner, Mom. I just met him." And there were a few other obstacles. Like the one where Lauren had to get her algae back to save her career before he got it to save his.

"Don't forget the Professor's birthday next week."

"I won't, Mom." And then another thought occurred to her. "Why do you call Dad that? Instead of Dale?"

"Because your dad *is* a professor."

"But he's also your husband. And my dad. Why do we

call him by his job?" It had never bothered her before, but for some reason, this morning, that title rankled.

"You call me Mom, and that's my job," her mother said.

"But that's…that's your name to me. You're more than your job."

"Oh, Lauren, you're thinking too much. Go fix your lab, cure some diseases, and make a name for yourself."

But after they hung up, she wondered. Did her mom really think that all she had was her job as wife and mother? And that all her father had was his job as a professor? Her mother had encouraged her to pursue her plan to become a scientist, had helped with every science fair project and book report, never taking over, but always offering ideas and asking the right questions at the right time, but Lauren had always wondered…did her mother resent Lauren's opportunity?

She supposed at the moment, it didn't really matter. What mattered was getting her own career back on track.

She looked longingly at the couch, and the remote, which would easily suck her into her preferred Sunday routine of flipping from the Food Network to *Hoarders: Buried Alive* marathons and back again. Instead, she downed the last of her tea and went to get dressed. Her lab wasn't going to reassemble itself.

A half hour later, as she pulled into the parking lot at Tucker U, Lauren noticed Evan getting off of his bike in front of the Biological Sciences building. He wore the whole cycling-guy get-up—skin-tight shirt covered in racing logos, snug shorts with extra padding in the butt area, skinny little shoes.

As she got out of her car, she watched him take off his

helmet, and with one shake of his head, his hair laid right back in place. Bizarre. Even if she wore her own hair an inch long, she'd have to spend fifteen minutes in the bathroom trying to smush everything back in place after sweating with a helmet on. Although he didn't look sweaty, either. He made the geeky-jock-professor thing look as effortless as his brother did the hot maintenance man/secret undercover guy.

Evan saw her approach and smiled. He really was a nice man. Cute in his extreme dorkiness, but he didn't do it for her. Not the way Mike did.

"Good morning, Dr. Kane," he said, pulling his ID badge from his backpack and running it through the scanner. He held the door for her, and she entered in front of him. The halls echoed with the absence of students.

"Thanks, Evan. Did you already take your big ride for the week?"

"Yes, I rode twenty-five miles this morning, and now I'm going to spend some time with the FUCR Frogs."

She grinned, her automatic response whenever Evan's research animals were mentioned. He returned the smile, apparently finally accepting that the acronym for the species of tree frog he worked with was really...*fucking*...funny.

"So are you just here to feed the little....uh...FUCRs, or will you be around all day?" She hadn't given it much thought before leaving the house, but the labs were even more deserted on Sundays than on Saturdays, and she felt a little dash of heebie-jeebies creeping in, especially after her little run-in with those people on the street last night.

"I'll be here for a couple of hours, but I'm hosting my brothers for our supposedly regular family dinner this evening, so I have a pork roast to prepare."

That brought Lauren's thoughts to a screaming halt. "Family dinner? That's nice." Surprising, too, given that the guys didn't seem to get along particularly well, but nice.

"Just before our grandmother died, she made us swear to have dinner together at least once a month." He turned the key in his door lock. "None of us will admit it—at least not to each other—but I think we're all a little afraid she'll come back and haunt us if we don't make an effort to get along. She was a practicing Catholic, but she's got roots that go way back into the snake-handling hills of Kentucky." He wiggled his eyebrows and disappeared into his lab.

Laughing, she unlocked her door, wishing that she'd had the opportunity to meet Grandma Gibson. It would have taken a heck of a woman to raise such strong-minded and different boys after their parents died.

Lauren continued into her own lab and looked around. It was still a mess, but she'd managed to get enough done yesterday that she could start cooking up another batch of algae. She was tempted to forget the whole thing. There was no way she'd be able to get the Pemberton group to give her an extension. She might as well start packing up her lab coats.

Instead, she found one of the big flasks she used as a growing chamber and rinsed it with distilled water, then took a vial of algae from the freezer and stuck it into her pocket before mixing up two liters of her homemade pond water. Then she found a blank notebook and recorded the date and vial number. It was official. She was a compulsive scientist. She'd probably take the stuff home and grow it in her garage if she couldn't work in the lab.

Huh. She *was* a scientist, through and through.

Not like her mom. Her mom liked science. Maybe even loved it. But she wasn't incomplete without it. If Lauren ran out of money, she'd find a way to keep going. If she got married and had sixteen kids and lived on the side of a mountain with no indoor plumbing, she'd find a way to keep going. If she got married…

Oh hell, no. She didn't have time to think about that right now.

Holding the vial up to the window to make sure it was thawed, she unscrewed the cap with one hand and carefully transferred the contents to the flask. She shoved a sterilized cork with two long glass tubes into the top and plugged in the aerator. There. In a little while, she'd feed the algae, and maybe get home in time to catch a couple of episodes of *Hoarders.*

She'd sort some more slides while she waited and try not to think about Mike Gibson's lips. Or any other part of his that she was inclined to kiss. Or lick. Or…

She snapped on the radio to distract herself.

But gosh, she really, really liked him. It was weird. She'd started thinking about everything in terms of Mike. Evan was making a pork roast tonight. She wondered if Mike cooked anything that fancy, or if he was all hamburgers on the grill and a container of potato salad.

Aaaaand there she went. Just because she'd realized she could probably still manage a career and a love life didn't mean she could manage a love life with a guy like Mike Gibson. Or that, late-night condom runs aside, it was unlikely a guy like Mike Gibson would want that with her. He would want the big city and big adventures, bad-guy-chasing adrenaline highs and stiletto-wearing sex goddesses. Not bookish, cat-loving, sneaker-wearing homebodies like Lauren. Though she might like to try out the sex goddess thing for a while.

Wow. She was really getting ahead of herself. Not a safe place to be.

The song on the radio ended, and a teaser for the news played. "Local police are warning that a dangerously addictive new drug called Devil's Dust may come in a less purified—but more deadly—form. A smokable alternative is rumored to be hitting the streets, with devastating effects. An unnamed person was admitted to University Hospital with severe neurological symptoms after smoking what he told doctors was a new experimental drug. And it's quite possibly being produced in a lab at a tri-state college. That story and more after these messages…"

Lauren sat up. *No.* Surely whoever had her drug wasn't smoking the algae. When she filtered the algae to dry it for storage, she'd mixed it with a poison that was bound to the cell walls. This caused the cells to release all of the drug so that when she made it into step two, she could rehydrate it and strain out the cell bodies and be left with only the drug. The poison stayed bound to the cell walls after the step two was released—but if someone was smoking the algae before it was rehydrated and rinsed, they would inhale the toxin.

Hadn't Mike asked her if the drug could be smoked? She'd hoped until now that he'd been wrong, that they'd find out this was a wild goose chase. The goose had just turned and pulled a gun.

"Dr. Kane."

Lauren looked up. Evan stood in the doorway, his face pale and rigid. "What is it?" Could he have heard the same news she had? She was glad to see him, though. Maybe she could talk this through with him, get him to help her figure out how this was all some weird misunderstanding.

Her momentary relief at his appearance fled the second he stepped into the lab, followed by her department head, Dr. Jerrold. What on earth was he doing in the building on a Sunday? She saw a uniformed campus security officer standing in the hall behind them.

Dr. Jerrold's normally round, smiling face was gray and serious. "Lauren, we need to have a word with you."

"Of course." Lauren nodded. She shot another glance at Evan, but he wouldn't meet her eye. "Evan, why are you here?"

Evan cleared his throat. "Witness."

A wave of fear spread through Lauren's body.

Dr. Jerrold said, "I've been in a teleconference with the chairman of the Pemberton Group."

"On a Sunday?" Her stomach churned. Whatever was coming, it was going to be bad.

"Apparently, this drug that's going around—this Devil's Dust—" He cleared his throat, then continued. "Someone on the Pemberton board is also on staff at the University of Cincinnati Medical Center, and they've spoken with the authorities. Seems they'd heard the drug is coming from Tucker University."

Lauren flashed on the email from Pemberton that she'd ignored last night. What if it hadn't been a reminder notice? What if they had been looking for an explanation from her about her drug hitting the streets?

"I don't know if you saw the morning news—"

She waved a hand, interrupting Dr. Jerrold. "I just heard

something on the radio—"

"There was a photograph of this substance that people are smoking. Lauren, it's your algae pellets."

She collapsed onto the stool. Her mind spun. How could this be real?

Evan stepped toward her. "Are you okay?"

She shook her head, then took a deep breath. "I didn't have anything to do with this," she said.

Dr. Jerrold smiled sadly. "I hope not. But Lauren, we have to take your lab keys and escort you from the building. Until further notice, the contents of your lab and all electronic information are off limits to you and any employee or student associated with your project."

"What? Why?"

"As you know, the Pemberton Group funds not only your research project, but that of several other faculty members at Tuck U. Pemberton is threatening to pull all of their support immediately unless we disassociate you from the department, pending investigation of your involvement with the Devil's Dust issue."

"So, am I fired?"

Dr. Jerrold shook his head. "Not if you're innocent. But until we have proof that you're not involved, you'll have to leave the Tucker University campus immediately."

Well, crap on a cracker. She was so screwed.

Chapter Fifteen

Mike checked his phone on the way into the grocery store. He had just enough time to get the stuff he needed to make cheesy potatoes for dinner at Evan's. He hoped that Dylan was actually going to show up to eat them. The kid hadn't come home last night but had texted that he was staying with a friend and would see Mike at Evan's later.

His choices for a shopping cart were between the one that looked like it had been drooled on—or worse—by every toddler in Tucker, and the one with a wonky front, right wheel. He chose the one with the wobbly wheel, because the tub of disinfecting wipes by the door of Food Giant was empty. Besides, fighting with a recalcitrant shopping cart gave him something substantial to wrestle. Something besides his own frustration.

It had been a long day of leaving voicemails, being on hold, and being ignored.

Mike had wanted to blow up Dylan's phone, insisting

on a meeting to get to the bottom of Dylan's involvement in the Devil's Dust situation, but Mike had wanted to get some more information from the task force in Cincinnati before he levied any more accusations at Dylan. The problem with *that* plan was that some of Lauren's dried algae pellets had hit the street overnight—and sent a couple of people to the hospital, and the investigators were up to their eyebrows in dead-ends. He'd finally spoken with his old partner, Dan, who'd reluctantly shared that no one knew where the two kids who were in the hospital had gotten the stuff, and they weren't talking. They might not be talking ever again.

And now he'd managed to arrive right in the middle of the Sunday afternoon grocery shopping happy hour. Who knew everyone in Tucker did their shopping at the same time?

His breath caught and his hands tightened on the handle of the cart when he noticed Lauren Kane. She didn't notice him, which was good, because he stopped in his tracks and just…looked at her. An elderly man elbowed him out of the way, with a smirk and a "She's a purty one," as he went by.

Lauren was intent on snagging something from the ice cream cooler, balancing a rather large bottle of pink wine, an economy-size bag of salt and vinegar potato chips, Oreo cookies, and a box of Pizza Rolls. Wearing baggy faded jeans and an Ohio State Buckeyes hoodie, she tried to use her shoulder to brush a stray strand of hair out of her eyes. Before he knew what he was doing, Mike moved forward and took the bottle and the Pizza Rolls from her before she dropped them. And so he wouldn't be tempted to stroke that hair out of her face. "I'll share my cart with you if you tell me why you're going on a suicide junk food feeding frenzy," he said.

After such a crappy day so far, it was both stunning and refreshing to see her here, doing something as mundane as grocery shopping, because Lauren wasn't the least bit mundane. She was energy and light and…he was in so, so deep.

She turned to look at him, and he saw that she also held a large, red apple under her chin. "I have an apple." She put the wine next to his bag of frozen hash browns. "And I don't have anything resembling cheese that doesn't need to be re-frigerated." She pointedly put the cookies next to his block of Velveeta.

"My grandmother lived to be eighty-four and she ate Velveeta every day," Mike said, taking the potato chips from her so she could get the tub of salted caramel ice cream she'd been chasing when he found her.

Lauren started to speak, then snapped her mouth shut.

Mike laughed. He was glad to see her. "Yeah, she prob-ably could have made it another twenty years, but she went out happy and full of her favorite tater casserole."

"That's nice," Lauren said, her expression soft. "You must miss her."

Mike felt a little tightening in his throat. He coughed.

The ice cream landed next to the economy-size tubs of butter and sour cream he needed for his casserole. "Thanks," she said, shaking out her fingers. "I was getting a hand cramp." She didn't meet his eyes, pretending to look for something between the frozen peas and brussels sprouts.

"So…What's going on?" He hoped she wasn't uncom-fortable seeing him after what had transpired between them last night. He *hoped* she might be a little glad to see him, too.

"Did you see the news today?" she asked.

"Yeah, I was gonna call, but…" He was gonna call, but hadn't known what to say. *Hey, I see that another piece of your research project is out there making people sick?* No, he hadn't planned to call her until he had something to tell her, like that he'd found the connection and made sure they were behind bars.

She fiddled with the strap of her purse. "Some kids are in the hospital from smoking those step one pellets. That's even worse than the purified step two because of that toxin I mixed in."

The pain in her eyes was a knife to his gut. "I know. I'm sorry." Goddamn it.

She looked at him then. "What am I supposed do? This is my fault. If I hadn't been so anxious to get more step two from the algae, I wouldn't have mixed in the cell membrane disruptor—"

He cut her off by pulling her into his arms right there in the middle of the Food Giant on Sunday afternoon. He held her, trying to show her with the strength of his body that he wouldn't let her fall apart. After a second, he pushed her away a little so he could see her face. "We're going to get these assholes. I promise." He hoped. "But first, you're going to come to my house and help me make Grandma's cheesy taters."

"For dinner with Evan and Dylan?"

"Hey—how did you—"

She gave him a watery smile. "I saw Evan at the lab this morning. I hear there's going to be pork roast, too."

For a moment, all he could do was stare into her eyes, then it hit him. He'd invited a woman home to dinner. His stomach clenched. Oh God, what had he done?

. . .

Mike looked in his rearview mirror to see if Lauren was still following him. After spending the afternoon together, trying to convince her that Velveeta was a miracle food, and that, even though it was kind of gummy, you *could* cut it with a knife, he wasn't sure she hadn't bailed on him. Who knew that someone so good with all those scientific instruments would be all thumbs in the kitchen? Mike was more than a little surprised that they hadn't ended up at the Tucker Community Hospital Emergency Room for wound care.

Instead, they'd spent a couple of hours laughing and talking and pretending that Lauren hadn't been suspended from her job, though they'd both jumped every time either of their phones buzzed with incoming emails, none of which had any news about the Devil's Dust or the smokable algae.

There were now two careers on the skids because of the Devil's Rangers. Mike prayed that he'd find something— anything—that proved that Dylan wasn't involved. The only thing he held on to at the moment was that he didn't have a living link between Dylan and the Rangers. Just circumstantial shit from the lab, which was pretty damned convincing.

When he saw Lauren connect gazes with him through the rearview mirror and wave, he proceeded down the next street. Evan lived in a little subdivision half a mile outside of the old city limits. Mike wasn't sure that Tucker had suburbs, but this area might qualify. The houses here were newer— 1980s—than the 1930s and 40s vintage in town. Mike turned his truck onto Evan's street just in time to see that same little black car from last night pull out of the driveway and speed past Lauren, who was parking a block up from Evan's house. The driver stared right at him, recognition shocking both of them. *Oh, hell no.* If he wasn't mistaken, that was Angela Romain. He thought about giving chase, but considering Dylan was standing, frozen, on Evan's front stoop, he didn't need to. He had his connection to the Devil's Rangers.

"God*damn* it." He threw the truck into park and grabbed the pan of potatoes. He thought about tossing the whole mess at his brother's head, but Lauren had caught up to him.

"What. The. Fuck." He stomped toward Dylan.

The kid stood his ground and met Mike's eyes. Lauren edged next to Mike, her presence the only thing keeping him from totally losing his shit. He already knew the answer, but he needed to know if Dylan would tell him the truth. "Who was that?"

"Angela."

Fuck. Fuck, fuck, *fuck*. "Angela."

"Yes," Dylan said.

"Angela Romain. Sister of Dino Romain, leader of the Devil's Rangers. Your ex-girlfriend. The one you promised me you'd broken up with ages ago."

"Mike, it's not—"

"How can it not be?" Mike paced. The front door opened, and Evan stepped out. "After everything we went through. After everything *you* went through with those assholes—"

"It's not like that!" Dylan was practically quivering with frustration, but Mike didn't give a shit.

"The one thing you swore to that judge was that you'd stay away from anyone associated with the Devil's Rangers!" He registered Evan standing in the doorway, arms crossed, and Lauren, looking between the three men. His mind raced. How had he so completely lost control of everything? His own life was one thing, but the family that he'd sworn to take care of was falling apart—had probably already shattered.

Evan didn't look as disturbed as Mike thought he should be, which raised his stress another couple of notches. He waved the pan of potatoes at the door, and a drop of oily cheese dripped from under the foil.

Evan's brow furrowed. "What are you talking about?" He came outside, looking for all the world like Mike was the crazy one, completely ignoring the splotch of food marring his perfect doormat. "Mike, come on inside. The neighbors—"

"Do you have any idea what's going on with Dylan?" Mike glared at him. How could he not know?

"Come on, let's all go inside," Evan commanded, holding the door and jerking his head at Dylan. "You, too."

Something in his tone… Mike had never known Evan to have a take-charge attitude outside of the lab.

Mike went inside. Rosemary and garlic perfumed the air, and something else…fresh, yeasty bread. A whiff of rationality slowed his heart rate—a little. Striding through the living room to the kitchen, he plunked the potatoes onto the counter next to the stove. Another drip. Lauren brushed past to grab a dishcloth from the edge of the sink and wiped up the mess as she scowled. He didn't blame her for being unhappy. He'd promised her not two hours ago that he was going to help her, and he was proving right now that he'd already let everything slip out of his control.

"You want to tell me what this is all about?" Evan asked.

"Maybe you should start. Did you know that Dylan was still involved with the Rangers?"

The look on Evan's face would have been worth a lot of money if he were in Hollywood, because he was a great actor. "What are you talking about?"

"You're letting him meet her here? Angela?"

"What?" Evan looked at Dylan, who had the grace to appear chagrined.

"It's really not what it looks like," Dylan said. "Angela's been helping me—"

"I know how she's been helping you," Mike interrupted. "Lauren caught her 'helping you' outside of her house last night, didn't she? What were you doing? Waiting for Lauren to go to sleep so you could go steal more of her drugs?"

"No, Mike, that's not what we were doing. And if you'd just listen—"

"I'm done listening. You're going to call whoever you've been working with, and we're going to go meet them and—"

"We're not going to do anything right now," Evan said. "Nothing but sit down and eat dinner."

"You've got to be kidding me," Dylan said, staring at his brother. "I'm not staying here to pretend to be a nice, happy family."

For once, Mike agreed with Dylan. "You can keep the potatoes," he told Evan. "I think Dylan and I need to go take care of some things."

"Mike, can I have a minute?" Lauren wrapped her hand around his arm and tugged.

Because he knew he was about to blow and needed to count to ten, he backed away from Dylan and followed her down the hall. When they were around the corner, he said, "What?"

Brown eyes filled with concern, she stroked her hand

down his arm and said, "I think you might want to back off a little, give this some space."

He shook her off—mostly because her touch felt too good. "Not your problem." Which was, he realized as soon as it was out of his mouth, the wrong thing to say, but he didn't have the time to rephrase it nicely.

"Seriously?" she asked.

"Yeah. I got this." He would have to find a way to take care of this for her. He'd failed to keep Dylan safe and out of trouble, but he did recognize that Lauren had a major stake in this situation.

"Dylan, wait!" Evan called just as the front door slammed.

"Stay here. I've got to talk to him." Mike turned away from Lauren, but not before he saw the hurt cross her features.

He opened the front door to follow Dylan into the fading light.

Behind him he heard Lauren call out, "Damn it, Mike! Wait for me!"

But he was already gone.

• • •

Lauren looked at Evan after the door slammed behind Mike. "He left me here!" She caught herself before she stomped her foot, but *Jeez*! She'd followed Mike home, indulged part of her fantasy that involved a hot guy in an apron—the cooking part—then had come over to his brother's to have a family meal, only to watch him flip out at his baby brother and take off. Some date. That is, if you could call it an actual *date* if you'd been picked up in the frozen food section of the Food Giant.

Evan sighed and lifted the corner of the foil covering the casserole dish. "Would you like to join me for dinner?"

"What? Aren't you going to go after them?" Lauren was aghast. Her...uh...almost boyfriend? Sort-of lover? Her guy-who-spent-an-otherwise-shitty-day-making-her-laugh? Anyway, whoever, or whatever Mike was to her had just run out of the house, chasing after the brother he'd accused of drug dealing, and Evan was just going to sit down and eat like nothing had happened.

"I'm sure Michael will handle himself with the appropriate restraint." Evan led the way to the kitchen, dropping Mike's casserole on the already-set dining room table on the way. He took two wine coolers from the refrigerator and unscrewed the lids, handing one to Lauren.

She thought about the previous night, when Mike had shown up at her door looking for Dylan. "So…"

He shrugged. "Dylan will probably call this Angela person, they'll do whatever it is that young lovers do to pass the time." Eye roll. "And Michael will calm down and get to the bottom of the dilemma."

An ugly feeling stole over Lauren. She took a long slug of wine cooler. "You act like this happens a lot. If Mike is so volatile, why does Dylan live with him?"

Evan leaned back against the counter, tipping his own bottle, staring off into the distance. "Michael is not volatile. He reacts to danger. He's...a rescuer, a fixer."

That was what she'd thought before they'd gotten here. It was the vibe she'd gotten from him, at least until fifteen minutes ago. She was glad she hadn't been totally off base. But… "You warned me away from him earlier."

He put his drink on the counter, rubbed his face, then

said, "Mike isn't someone I could see with an academician, such as yourself. I suppose I was trying to look out for you. But perhaps it's best I stay out of your personal life. Although…I can see how *you* might be awfully good for *him*."

"Oh," she said, not sure what to say. "Um…"

He waved away her discomfort. "Let's eat. Dylan's safe with Michael. He'd take a bullet for anyone he cares about." He grabbed the pork roast and put the meat on the table next to the cheesy potatoes.

"And you wouldn't?"

Evan returned to the kitchen and reached into a drawer, pulling out a serving spoon. "I can't say that I have ever had—or am likely to have—the opportunity. But Mike is the brother with physical courage, while I'm the rational one. When our grandmother died, she left me as executor of her estate and Mike as legal guardian of Dylan until he reached eighteen. She was a wise woman."

Lauren took the spoon from Evan and followed him back into the formal dining room. She sat, then poked the spoon into the steaming casserole of potatoes while he carved the pork roast.

"Why do you think that?" Lauren wondered why she was so focused on this issue when her own life was falling apart. Maybe because it was easier than to think about the fact that the thread supporting her career had frayed beyond repair, and it was just waiting for the breeze that would send it plummeting into obscurity.

Evan sat down and served each of them a fragrant slice of meat. "When we were kids, Mike was the one who took the blows for both of us when Dylan's father found fault. I was the one who hid in the closet. On the other hand, I was the one who came up with the explanations for the teachers and Grandmother about how Michael had fallen out of a tree or tripped over a skateboard."

"Oh," Lauren said, feeling like she should say something more profound but unable to find words. Evan simply waved his fork at the potatoes and said, "Eat your dinner."

Her stomach growled. Might as well. After all, it wasn't like she had anything better to do…like find her missing drugs and save her career.

Chapter Sixteen

After sharing what had to be the most delicious—albeit artery-blocking—cheesy potatoes and pork roast, and a rather awkward dinner conversation with Evan, Lauren stopped at the convenience store a few blocks from her house to pick up a bottle of white wine and some chocolate. She'd left her previous grocery purchases in Mike's house. She felt like a cliché. Depressed and stressed, she'd go home and overeat and over-drink and worry about Mike, driving around somewhere on a mission to find his brother, bring down a drug cartel, get his job back, leap over a couple of tall buildings in a single bound...

Unfortunately, she was afraid that his quest for redemption was going to come with the price of his brother's freedom. It was looking more and more like Dylan was involved in the destruction of Lauren's lab and the theft of her drug. How could he not be? She'd been defending the kid, but the coincidences were starting to mount.

She tried calling Dylan a couple of times herself, on her way out of Evan's neighborhood, hoping that—what? That she could ask him where his girlfriend's gangster brother's hideout was so she could show up, sneak in, steal back her algae pellets and the purified Devil's Dust—er, step two—so no one else got hurt, and oh yeah, maybe she could still make enough of the step three drug in time for her meeting with the Pemberton Group? And Dylan would just go, "You're right, Dr. Kane. Here, let me text you the address to Dino the Gangster Dude's hideout."

Her gut still pleaded for Dylan to be innocent, but her gut was also telling her to grab hold of Mike Gibson with both hands—and thighs—and keep him with her forever— and she *knew* that was a bad idea.

Thanking the clerk, she pocketed her change and thought of Mike, in here last night, buying condoms. He'd been buying condoms to come back to her house and use them.

She doubted that would ever happen now. Was it wrong that she was thinking about how much she wanted to get naked with Mike instead of worrying about how useless she was when it came to saving her career? The neighbors were all inside when Lauren turned onto her quiet little street. Nothing moved but the headlights of a car—a black car—that was pulling out of her driveway. As it disappeared around the corner at the other end of the street, the bass sound of rap music faded into the twilight. Dread crept over her shoulder and wrapped around her heart with icy fingers.

When Lauren pulled into her driveway, she noticed a cat-colored mound on her porch. Was that Kevin? She got out of her car and locked it, tucking the bag of wine and chocolate under her arm.

"Kevin?" The mass of fur didn't move. Surprising, since Kevin didn't like loud cars. He normally hid under the bushes. He must be pissed at her. He ignored her sometimes, if she'd left him outside for too long without his dinner. But this was different. He wasn't acknowledging her...he wasn't even..." Oh my God." He wasn't breathing. Someone had—

She turned away and vomited over the porch railing.

After she'd emptied her stomach and her head stopped spinning, she backed off of the porch, careful not to look directly at Kevin's lifeless body. She avoided stepping on him and pulled her phone from her pocket. She punched in 911.

"Someone murdered my cat on my front porch," she told the operator after identifying herself and giving her address.

"Ma'am, I'm afraid that's not an emergency. I can refer you to animal control, if you'd like."

What? Her cat was dead! "But those guys in the loud car... They..."

"Did someone threaten you?"

"There was a car in my driveway. A loud car." That sounded lame. But... "I'm scared," she admitted. "I think they were looking for me. And poor Kevin—my cat—he's dead."

The operator said something to someone in the background. "Ma'am, there's a patrol car in the neighborhood. We can ask him to stop by. Are you inside the house?"

"No, I just got home. I was going to have dinner with my boy—with some friends, and—" She was rambling. "I should go in through the back door."

"No, ma'am. Please, just stay outside on the sidewalk until the officer gets there."

"Okay," Lauren said. That made sense. Don't go inside. She knew that. Her knees were shaking, and she needed— "Can you ask them to bring me some gum?"

"Huh?"

"I threw up and my mouth is gross."

Before she sat down on the grassy patch dividing the sidewalk from the street, Lauren unscrewed the cap of the bottle of wine. She swished a mouthful around and spit it into the grass, then took a big slug and swallowed before sitting down to wait for the officers. Maybe she could get a decent buzz on before she had to tell the police that the brother of the man she was falling in love with had something to do with her murdered cat and had maybe stolen a bunch of deadly drugs.

* * *

When Mike got the call from Crawford, he'd just pulled back into his own driveway. Heart racing, he backed out and turned toward Lauren's side of town. Crawford had been in the station when Lauren had reported that her cat had apparently been killed by some thugs in a black car. Considering the drug thefts and the threatening message left on her lab wall, the police were treating this as slightly more than an act of animal cruelty.

The police were already at her house, he reminded himself when he was tempted to break traffic laws. She was safe. He had time.

No, he didn't have time. He needed to be with her. He didn't know what the hell was going on. His little brother, the brother he'd sworn to protect, was involved with a drug ring, and there didn't seem to be anything Mike could do to stop Dylan from complete self-destruction. He'd run away from Mike after leaving Evan's house, disappearing into the evening gloom between some houses. The only thing Mike could figure was that he'd had Angela come pick him up somewhere, and they were off commiserating about what an asshole Mike was.

One thing he was sure of, which gave him a reason to keep going, was that Lauren Kane was good, and honest, and for some crazy reason, she liked him. Or she had, before he'd made an ass of himself in front of her and left her at Evan's house.

He squealed to the curb and barely got the keys out of the ignition before he jumped out and slammed the door. Lauren, Crawford, and a uniformed cop looked up at him as he pounded past the patrol car parked in front of her little bungalow.

Lauren sat on the grass with a blanket draped around her shoulders. She turned a pale face and big eyes on him. He thought she relaxed a little as he walked toward her. He knew he felt better, seeing her there, safe and reasonably calm. She cradled a half-empty wine bottle to her chest and spoke around an enormous wad of gum. "Hi. What are you doing here?"

He looked at Crawford, who shrugged and said, "I just got here, too. I didn't tell her I called you."

"You called him?" Lauren bestowed a huge smile on Crawford. "That was really nice."

"Are you drunk?" Mike asked.

"I think I might be, a little. I was kinda freaked out when I got home and found…" She trailed off, and the smile morphed into the forerunner of an apocalyptic meltdown. "My cat is — and I don't know — "

"Lauren, it's okay. I can help if you let me." He squatted next to her.

"I'm not so sure about that." She prepared to tip the bottle to her lips again.

Mike took it from her. "Let me hang on to that until we're done with the police, okay?"

"Oh." She looked at the uniformed cop. "Tony, you wouldn't write me a ticket, would you? These are extenuating circumstances, right?"

"I think that, as long as you wait to finish that until later, we can let the open container charge slide this time." The officer suppressed a smile before walking away.

Lauren wobbled to her feet. Mike rose, steadying her. She took a step forward, and then wrapped her arms around Mike's waist, surprising him. She had to be loaded, because the last time he'd seen her, she'd looked ready to murder him. He tentatively put his arm around her shoulders and tucked her against him.

"I'm sorry," she said into his shirt.

"What are you sorry for?"

"I have to tell you something bad."

Chapter Seventeen

Lauren woke up with her face smushed against something hot and hard, something like a denim-covered tree trunk.

"Hey, there you are."

She blinked at a big naked foot propped on a coffee table next to an empty white zinfandel bottle. There was a television a little farther out, with some sort of sepia-toned gangster movie playing softly. This was *not* her place, most definitely. In fact, that was Miss Posy, er…Possum, sitting on the floor next to the TV, alternately grooming herself and growling. Huh. Mike's cat looked better. Her hair was already starting to fill in the bald patches she'd gnawed into her skin at the shelter.

Lauren realized she'd been sleeping on Mike's thigh. Which meant the back of her head was right next to… "Oh, boy." She sat up too quickly, her head spinning. She focused on the streetlight that she could see through his living room window, shining through the night and anchoring her.

"Are you gonna be sick?"

"Um. No?"

He snort-laughed. She was afraid to turn and look at him, to let him see the pillow marks—well, the leg marks—that no doubt creased her face. She wiped at the side of her mouth, sneaking a look down at his lap to make sure she hadn't drooled on him.

One of his hands came up to the back of her neck, under her hair. He gave her a quick caress and then stood.

"You want something to drink?" Without waiting for an answer, he walked to the fridge in the little kitchen that she could see through a doorway. He pulled out a Diet Coke and a bottle of water, which he carried back to her. He even unscrewed the cap, which was thoughtful, because her hands weren't ready to do anything so complicated yet.

She took a long drink, then finally looked at him.

He gazed back at her. "You okay?"

She tried to smile reassuringly. "I think so." She tasted the inside of her mouth. Not too bad. They'd gone to the Quick Stop on the way from her house to his and bought her a toothbrush, which seemed to have warded off hangover breath. "I don't usually drink very much," she finally said.

"Yeah, I guessed that."

She scooted over a little bit and he sat back down, put his arm around her, and pulled her against him. There was tension in his embrace.

"Do I smell icky?"

His nose brushed her hair away from her neck and he inhaled, sending a shiver along her spine and heat to the rest of her. "Nope."

"Oh. My." She vaguely remembered telling him that she

thought Dylan was the bad guy. He'd taken it fairly calmly, but she figured that was because he already believed the worst.

She'd wanted to finish her wine on the way to Mike's house, and she vaguely remembered telling him he was the sexiest control freak she knew after he'd taken it from her and screwed the top on, tucking it into the tool box in the bed of his truck for the ride home. When they'd gotten inside, she pushed him down onto the couch, and then climbed on top of him, straddling him, leaning for a kiss before remembering that she'd thrown up less than an hour earlier. At which point, she thought, but wasn't sure, she'd burst into tears and run into the bathroom to use her new toothbrush.

She sat up, pulling away. "Oh, God. Well, at least I didn't drunk-text you. I didn't, did I?"

"Nope. Just drunk-groped me, but my virtue is still intact."

She smiled at that, then the rest of it came rushing back to her. "My cat's dead. Murdered."

He nodded. "I'm really sorry about that."

"Thanks." She was quiet then, not sure what to say.

"Crawford texted me a little while ago. He said he'd have someone check around off and on all night to keep an eye on things around your house until morning. They went inside but couldn't tell if anything was taken."

"What about…Kevin?"

"He took care of him, too. Crawford will show you where he's buried in the back yard later, if you want."

"I wish I could figure out who's doing this. If someone wants my drugs, I get that, but why hurt Kevin? He was innocent. This feels…personal. I know I said I think Dylan might actually be involved, but I can't believe he'd do *that*."

"He's not alone in this. And the other people, other Devil's Rangers? They'd do anything to get what they want." He paused. "Do you have anything at your house? Anything from work?"

"Just some notebooks and my laptop. But that stuff isn't going to make any sense to anyone without an organic chemistry or pharmacology background."

"Someone who also knows a lot of biology."

"What? Like who?"

Mike was staring at her. Did he think…?

"Surely you're not thinking it could be Evan, are you? I mean, yeah, he's got the background. Heck, even if he didn't, he's smart enough to figure it out. But it's not *Evan*."

Mike paced to the window and pulled down a slat on the shade, let it go, and walked back across the room. "I don't really think so, either. Just throwing ideas out there. Besides, Evan's always been the good brother."

She remembered what Evan had revealed to her yesterday, about how Mike had taken so many licks for him. She imagined Mike as a teenager, angry, protective, scared but standing up for his siblings anyway. "Evan doesn't think he's the good one," she said.

Ignoring that, he asked, "Does Dylan have enough science under his belt to take your algae stuff and make it into the drug?"

"Probably," Lauren said, but something was tickling the back of her brain. She just couldn't grasp it. She needed to get home and look at her laptop. "I should go."

"Where are you going to go?" He took his hand away from his neck.

"I've imposed on you enough, and I— I have to go home and see if anything was taken. Maybe that will help me figure out who did it. You don't have to take me, I can call the Night Walk van." That was a program the women's student association had so that no one had to walk around campus in the dark alone. They would make off campus trips, if it was within a few blocks of campus, too.

"The hell you are. You're not going home alone."

"It's okay. I can go by myself."

"And I can take you. If you've really got to go right this minute."

Did he want that? Or was he just being nice again? She didn't want him to hang around with her just because he felt obligated. She wasn't going to be another responsibility that he had to take care of. Besides, she was on a roll. No big, strong, he-man was going to tell her what to do. "No, I'm fine, I'll just call— "

"Why not?" He was mad now. Sparks practically shot from his eyes.

"Because…because… God, because I want you to go with me so much, and I can't ask you to help me!"

And then his arms were around her, and he was kissing the mad, crazy confusion right out of her.

His lips, and teeth, and tongue met her lips, and teeth, and tongue and sent every thought of not needing him straight to hell. She wrapped her arms around his shoulders, and his big, hot muscles flexed under her hands as he ran one hand up her back, under her hair, and the other down over her backside, gripping the back of her thigh.

He yanked her leg up around his waist, and she gave a little hop, then wrapped her other leg around him as he pressed her body into the door behind her, aligning every-thing, pushing his erection against her, hard heat nudging through layers of denim, trying to get where he was sup-posed to be.

And that was the thing, wasn't it? Getting him inside her was all she needed. That would solve the mysteries of the universe, wouldn't it?

Mike ended the kiss and pulled back, staring into Lau-ren's eyes, chest heaving with a shakiness that moved some-thing deep within Lauren, something that wasn't a repro-ductive organ, something that felt curiously like her heart, cracking open to let in this man, this dark, complicated man full of secrets, this man who wanted her. *Her*. He wanted her. And God help her, she wanted him.

• • •

"So," Mike said, breathing heavily against Lauren's lips. He felt her heat through their jeans and groaned but managed to get out, "I've got a brand-new box of condoms." He heard his own voice crack. He had to get inside her.

She shifted, pressing against him, rising up and then down a little, and moaned. "I don't—" she gasped. "I think maybe—"

He headed down the hall, holding her legs around his waist, her arms around his neck. He stopped a couple of times to kiss her, tongues tangling, pressing against her, so desperate to be inside her that he was almost capable of do-ing it through layers of denim.

But they'd been there before. This time was going to be the real thing.

"Put me down," she told him when they got as far as the hall bathroom door.

"I don't want you that far away from me," he told her.

"I want to be in your bed as soon as possible, and if you put me down, we have a better shot of making it before I spontaneously combust."

He laughed as he let her slide down his body until her feet were on the floor. It felt good. God, he loved this woman.

His brain froze for an instant, then his heart pushed hot blood through. He couldn't be in love. Could he? Whatever it was he felt, it was good, and he could worry about it later. "When you go up in flames, it's not going to be spontaneous. It's gonna be because I sent you there, one stroke at a time."

They made it to his bedroom, and he started pulling at her clothes while she was pulling at his. Their hands tangled as they reached for one another's waistbands at the same time.

It nearly killed him, but he stepped back from her. "I'll do me, you do you."

"Oh, God. The visual I just got of that…" she said.

Which made him have the same visual. Or at least, the counterpoint. *Jesus.* "Maybe next time. Right now…"

He pulled his jeans down. His aching cock sprang free as she revealed her tiny red panties, and then the dark triangle beneath. She stopped for a moment, looking at him, letting him look at her. "Wow," she said, reaching out to run her hand down his chest.

And didn't that make him feel ten feet tall.

"Shirt. Off. Now," he said.

After the briefest hesitation, she complied, ripping her top over her head and unhooking her bra in record time.

It was one of those front clasp things, and then her breasts were there for his viewing, his touching pleasure.

He stalked toward her, and she fell backward onto the mattress, then scooted back so that her head was almost at the other side of the bed. He landed on his knees, on the bed, and pulled her thighs apart. Holy hell. She was wet and swollen and he hadn't even touched her yet.

He moved back, and then fell to his belly, erection pressed between his stomach and the bed. He inhaled her scent and then looked up at her face. She watched him, eyes wide, lips parted, breath fast and shallow. Holding her gaze, he lowered his mouth to taste her. The sound she made, part cry, part groan, nearly made him come apart.

As he licked and sucked and nuzzled, she writhed against him. She put her hands in his hair, holding him against her. He smiled. She liked this. Her thighs tensed. She was ready. *He* was ready.

He rose and advanced up her body, kissing her belly, her ribs, the undersides of her breasts. The hands in his hair were still pulling, but it was to get him to move higher, faster.

He sat back, out of her reach, but she sat up, following him. She wrapped her arms around his neck and kissed him, her tongue diving into his mouth.

He unwrapped her arms and held both of her hands in one of his. "Hang on, babe."

"I need you," she said, but stilled, panting, her frustration clear.

He reached for one of the condoms he'd put on the nightstand and tore it open with his teeth. He had to let her go to roll the damned thing on, but then her hands were on him again.

Finished with the condom, he reached for her hands again, capturing them and pushing her back onto the bed. With one hand, he held her hands above her head, and with the other, he pulled her leg open so that he could position himself between her thighs.

Quiet, still now, she waited. He brushed against her slick folds. Even through the latex, he felt her heat, felt her quiver against him.

"You ready?" he asked. Please, God, let the answer be yes.

She nodded.

He entered her, just a fraction, and then forced himself to retreat.

"Please. Please, Mike, please. Just fuck me, for God sakes."

And that was it. He pushed into her and began to move. Inches from her face, because he was still holding her hands above her head, he stared into her golden eyes, so full of... his own reflection.

"Oh, oh, oh oooh!" she cried, and her spasms rocked him.

He moved faster and faster, feeling his whole world narrow into throbbing heat at the base of his spine before sensation exploded through him, sending the top of his head somewhere into the next county.

His last thought before he lost consciousness was that he should die now, because he wouldn't survive doing this again.

Chapter Eighteen

Lauren stifled a chuckle as Mike released her hands with a little snore after withdrawing from her body. He'd barely rolled them to their sides, and was, in fact, still mostly on top of her.

She took the opportunity to touch him and look at him up close. While he was completely relaxed, she felt energized and wide awake. But she was *too* comfortable, snuggled up against his naked heat, unable to move from beneath him.

And didn't *that* scare the living hell out of her.

She was crazy, over the top, skull over tarsals, in love with a man she'd known for less than a week. A take-charge, get-things-done, alpha man. Like Alex. But no, Alex had been a control freak. That was different. Wasn't it?

How had she gotten from trying to go home alone to naked with Mike and in love? She had no idea. She probably needed to get somewhere that her mind wasn't clouded with the sights, smells, and sound of a giant, sleeping, sex god. Somewhere that she wasn't tempted to crawl under the covers and use kisses and licks to wake the giant's, uh, beanstalk. After which, he would probably tell her again that she couldn't go home alone.

Lauren pushed at Mike's shoulder and he muttered something about "again soon," but gave her room to move. She rolled out of bed and scrambled for her clothes, then pulled the quilt up over Mike's sprawled nakedness and tiptoed into the hallway bathroom to dress. She had to get out of there. She'd seen a bicycle leaning against the garage in the backyard. She could borrow it and ride home.

"What are you doing?" Mike murmured.

She jumped. "Uh, leaving, actually," she said. Not slick, but hey—it was true.

He sat up, rubbing a hand across his jaw. "Huh? No, you're not."

See? He was bossy. That was the crux of the matter. "Yeah. I am."

"Where are you going?"

"I've got to… I need to get some things done."

"What things?"

"Just…things." She needed to go home and check on her house.

He stood, yanking the condom off and tying it in a knot before walking across the room to drop it in the trash can. "Give me a minute. I'll take you."

"No, you don't have to do that. I don't want you to do that."

He stopped on his way into the bathroom and turned halfway back toward her. She couldn't help but appreciate how nice he looked from behind. Michelangelo's David had nothing on Mike Gibson's back view.

"You can't go running off," he said, voice low and growly.

"I'm running off."

"What the fuck for?"

"Because...because you're not the boss of me." Oh, hell. She sounded like she did when her cousin Melanie had been in charge of babysitting her.

"Who said I was?"

"You just said I couldn't leave without you."

"Because you don't have a car here!"

"I can walk."

"I'm sure you can." He turned fully around then. *Oh, hell.* That old David statue was *way* underperforming compared to Mike's front view. He walked—no, *stalked*—toward Lauren.

She backed up, right against the wall.

He leaned over her, his full height and weight surrounding her, closing out the world, cocooning her in scent and warmth.

She pushed at his chest, but he didn't move. "See? You're overpowering me. You do that all the time!"

He stepped back then, stricken. "What are you talking about?"

Could he be that obtuse? "You—you—you're going to take over my world! You keep—rescuing me, like some stupid—hero guy—and I can't let you do that!"

"You said you liked it last night. I know you were a little buzzed, but when we left your house, you said—"

"Don't you get it?" She was yelling now. "I *did* like it! That's the whole damned problem!"

"What are you trying to say?"

"I'm saying, it's over. This thing between us, whatever it was, isn't going to continue. It can't. It doesn't work. *We* don't work." She softened her tone, not sure whether she was addressing him or herself when she said, "I'm sorry."

He stared at her for a moment, then said, "Don't be sorry. You're probably right. We don't work. Hell, I don't 'work' with anyone. No surprise there." He put his hands on his head, and tugged at his hair, then scrubbed his face with his hands. Without another word, he turned and walked away, shutting the bathroom door behind himself.

She couldn't decide if she was relieved or if her feelings were hurt that he didn't stay and wrestle her independence demons into submission. So she ran, letting herself out and grabbing Dylan's bicycle from its place against the garage wall.

Dawn's earliest glow was beginning to lighten the eastern sky as she pedaled across campus toward her own side of town, facing the realization that she had acted like a complete idiot. But *damn*. No one had ever twisted her up quite like that. Turned her upside down and inside out and made her question everything she'd thought she believed about herself and what her world was supposed to be.

Her world was supposed to be centered around a research lab and the classes she taught. She was supposed to come home at night and feed her cat and watch cable TV and maybe every now and then, hook up with some nice, boring guy who would be too distracted by the newest images from the Hubble Telescope to sneak out late at night to buy condoms, or volunteer to foster a neurotic cat, or show up every damn time she needed him, and even sometimes when she didn't want him.

In spite of herself, she half expected to hear Mike's truck rumbling along behind her and told herself that it was a good thing it wasn't.

She had to push thoughts of Mike out of her head. Focus on what was important in the here and now. Which meant finding out what had happened to her drugs. And who had killed her freaking cat. And she had to do it alone. Maybe if she could get to those pellets before Mike *and* the police, she could still save her own career—since that was all she had left now. But if Dylan was involved, maybe she could get him to confess, return her drugs, turn himself in…anything to minimize the possibility that Mike would have to be the one to drag the brother he was in charge of protecting into prison. She was so damned confused right now, she didn't know what she wanted, or what she needed as far as Mike was concerned, but she did know that she wanted him to be happy—and for Mike to be happy, his family had to be safe.

Fifteen minutes later, Lauren bumped over the curb and into her driveway. She rolled the bike around the side of the house. Unlocking the kitchen door, she stepped inside and went to look for her laptop.

She sneezed when she entered her bedroom. *Ugh*. She didn't have time to come down with a cold. Kneeling next to the bed, she leaned her head on the mattress as she reached underneath to where she stored her laptop, and sneezed again.

Her hand met only air. Oh God, no.

The notebooks she'd brought home from the lab and her laptop were missing. She rubbed her nose, crushed to realize that she was now certain that Dylan had been in her house, looking for her notes, because only his cologne seemed to trigger this much sneezing. She pulled out her phone and woke up the app that the IT security people had recently installed on her desktop at work and her portable device. The app that would tell her where her missing laptop had gone.

As her chest squeezed tight, she knew she was also about to prove Mike's biggest fears were accurate—that the younger brother he wanted to save was behind all the chaos and havoc. She just hoped she could find Dylan in time to save Mike from seeing it firsthand.

· · ·

Mike started to follow Lauren home, to make sure she got there safely, but decided at the last moment to give her—and himself—some space. He knew she'd be okay at her house, that Crawford was sending a patrol past every thirty minutes or so.

The sound of Dylan's bike brakes squealing around the corner as she'd ridden away echoed in his brain. The house echoed with her absence. He didn't know what he could have done differently, how he could have made her stay.

Trying to *make* her stay was part of the problem, he understood that much. And why wouldn't it be? She was a smart, successful professional, a woman who didn't need a man to make her complete. And he was a washed up ex-cop with a desperate need to fix things that he couldn't fix—not his brother, not his job, and not Lauren's project. He rubbed the center of his chest. There was something in him that he couldn't fix, either. Maybe it was his heart. The more he cared, the harder he tried...the more fucked up everything got.

Even so, he was going to have to go after Dylan this morning. The fact that the kid hadn't come home last night was the last nail in the coffin of Mike's trust.

He found his keys and fired up the truck. After driving around for a while, he found himself at Tucker U. Jason was outside of the Bio building, doing something next to the trash can where the possums lived. With a start, Mike realized it was Monday morning. People were coming and going as though everything in the world was normal.

"Hey, I thought you were off today, since you worked on Saturday," Jason said by way of greeting.

Mike shrugged. "I was out and about. What are you doing?" He wasn't about to admit that he was feeling sorry for himself and scared for his brother and wanted a connection to at least one person who didn't find him lacking.

"Uh, I thought maybe we could make this a little nicer. You know, because Parent's Weekend is coming and everything." Jason stepped aside and Mike could see that the man had planted a couple of rose bushes next to the can and added a little rock wall that effectively camouflaged the trash can and gave the critters some steps into their home.

"Wow, dude, that's nice."

Jason looked a little embarrassed. "You're girlfriend's gonna like it. You can tell her you did it."

"She's not my girlfriend," Mike said. Whatever he and Lauren had between them—however briefly—was over. Once Mike busted Dylan and got the drugs off the street, she was going to be safe. She wouldn't need his help anymore, and she would be moving on.

"I think you might be wrong," Jason said.

"She doesn't want me," Mike said. "At any rate, she

shouldn't."

"Maybe you should let her decide that."

"What makes you so wise?"

Jason laughed. "I'm not wise, but I know about women. Thirty years ago, Louella Tucker, daughter of the richest woman in town, decided she wanted me. I tried to chase her off, but she kept coming. And look at us now."

Mike snorted. "You're the son-in-law of Miss Emmaline Tucker, and you work unclogging toilets and landscaping around trash cans."

"I don't have to do this job. I like this. I had a desk at Kentucky Jelly for exactly three months. I developed asthma from wearing a neck tie."

Before Mike could ask anything else, Evan burst through the front door of the Bio building, racing toward the parking lot. When he saw Mike, he pulled up short. "Thank God you're here. We have a problem."

Chapter Nineteen

Lauren followed the directions to the address that her laptop's GPS sent, wondering if she'd done the right thing by calling Evan to let him know where she was going. She didn't want to involve anyone, but she knew that if Dylan was in trouble, he'd need his family. And it might be selfish of her, but she didn't want to be the one responsible for making Mike catch Dylan with the step two drug and step one algae. Because as soon as she'd started sneezing, it was clear that Dylan had been in her house. And if he'd been in her house and taken her laptop, he had all the notes he'd need to go into Devil's Dust production on his own.

When Evan heard where Lauren was going, his responses were even more clipped and formal than normal. She thought about what he'd told her about hiding in the closet when he was a kid. Surely he was over that by now?

On the fifteen-minute drive into the country, Lauren's brain itched. There was something she was missing about this whole thing. She thought about the chemical she used, the one that would release the step two drug more easily. It was toxic—it was removed during purification, but until that step, it was bound to the algae cells. This was why the people who had smoked it had gotten so sick. Dylan knew about the toxin. He wouldn't have sold anyone the algae to smoke with that chemical on it, because even the greediest of drug dealers wouldn't kill off his customers. Someone who didn't know about the chemical had to be involved here. Was that what was bothering her?

A shiver of foreboding went down her spine. What if she found someone else with Dylan and her computer? She looked at her phone, thinking that maybe she should call Mike, after all. But after the way she'd run out on him this morning, he had to believe she was hysterical. And maybe there would be nothing at this address. Nothing but an abandoned, stolen computer. She'd just take a look around, and if things seemed too dangerous, she'd call Crawford and let him deal with it. She had 911 on speed dial.

The little red dot on the GPS was located just off State Route Fourteen, a rural road that ran between Tucker and Napier's Bend, no longer a thoroughfare since the interstate had gone in, but there were farms and a few houses spaced between stretches of forest.

She passed the turnoff once and had to backtrack to find the gravel drive leading to the old farmhouse on the side of the hill where the red dot seemed to be centered. She turned onto the drive and suddenly realized that she had no idea what she was doing. She'd left her house with some vague notion that she'd march out here and talk to Dylan like one rational adult to another, or at least like professor to student.

She got along well with Dylan and thought he liked her. But she didn't know this Dylan that she was coming to see. This Dylan, who had possibly lied to her, stolen her drugs, entered her house uninvited to steal her computer, maybe even killed her cat. She was worried about this Dylan.

The farmhouse was dark and still. Lauren put her SUV in park and sat for a minute, just watching to see if anyone came to the window. Nothing stirred. Maybe there was no one there. Maybe her computer was just sitting inside on the kitchen table, and she could go in and pick it up and leave—pretend like nothing had happened. She'd go home, call Chief Crawford, and tell him after the fact.

She craned her neck and could see the back end of a car just barely visible, pulled most of the way behind the house. With trepidation, Lauren got out of her car to get a better look. It looked like the black vehicle that she'd seen on her street the night that Mike had been at her house. The car with the Devil's Rangers emblem that Dylan and his girl-friend rode in. Was it the same one that had been pulling out of her driveway after Kevin was murdered?

Lauren dug her phone from her pocket and scrolled to the number she'd saved for Crawford. She thought about pushing "call" but hesitated. She'd come this far—she might as well knock on the door and try to speak to Dylan. He wouldn't hurt her. He might not give her what she came for, but she knew he wouldn't hurt her. Right?

God, she felt like an idiot for continuing to hope that he was somehow, miraculously, not involved. When he'd been at Evan's house, he—

She realized what had been tickling her mind. *Damnit!* At Evan's, Dylan hadn't smelled like that god-awful cologne he'd had on in the lab the other day. The cologne that was in her house, making her sneeze. How did it get there, then?

She jumped when a hand landed on her shoulder.

• • •

"Do you want me to drop you off at home?" Mike asked Evan. He didn't want to take the time, adrenaline pushing him to drive as fast as he could to the address Lauren had given Evan. But the instinct to protect this brother was present, pulsing below the need to get to Lauren and Dylan before someone got hurt.

"No, I'll stay with you."

"Are you sure? I can go by myself. I'm just going to go out there and—"

"And what, Mike? Take on the world all alone again?"

"What are *you* going to do?" he shot back. *Fuck.*

There was silence from the passenger seat.

"I'm sorry. That was a low blow," Mike said. "I—"

"I can call 911 if things go bad."

A glance in Evan's direction told Mike that he was resolved to come along. "Okay. Thanks."

Evan nodded.

After wrestling with his ego for four and a half seconds, Mike called Crawford to give him a heads up. Thirty seconds later, after Crawford filled him in, he was glad he did.

"What?" Evan asked once Mike had disconnected the call.

"The property is registered to Alex Barker."

"Oh, hell," Evan said.

Oh hell was right. What the heck was Lauren's ex-boyfriend doing with a remote piece of property where her stolen laptop now was?

"Did Dylan work with Barker when he was at Tuck U?"

"No. Alex Barker left the spring before you and Dylan returned to Tucker."

"Then why would Dylan have access to his property?"

"I didn't say Dylan didn't know him. Barker has returned several times over the past year or so, ostensibly to retrieve data he left on campus."

"Ostensibly." Mike loved it when Evan threw big words around.

"I believe he was actually attempting to rekindle the… uh…relationship he had with Dr. Kane."

Mike shook his head. He still had a hard time believing Lauren had been involved with that jerk.

"If it's any consolation," Evan continued, "Lauren seemed barely interested in him when they dated the first time. They had been co-workers in graduate school, and their families are friends. I suspect their…conjugation was based more on convenience than affection, at least on Lauren's part."

Mike's phone rang again. He answered it and listened to Crawford with a cold block of dread growing in his gut.

"What is it?" Evan asked when he'd hung up.

"Alex got fired from UC a few months ago, then made threats of retaliation against the dean, but the charges were dropped in exchange for a promise to stay off campus forever. And the son of a bitch has a record for stalking."

"Why did we not know this? He worked at Tucker for a year and a half." Evan pointed. "Turn right at the end of the street and then left on Tucker-Union road."

"Do they do criminal background checks on everyone?"

"No, I guess not. Just faculty."

"And he wasn't faculty?"

"Not officially. He was a post-doctoral fellow. But still. I think I'll bring this up at the next all-campus faculty meeting."

"You do that."

"You know, condescension doesn't suit you," Evan said tightly.

Mike sighed. Everything was so fucked up. He didn't need this. So he would put it to rest. "You're right. I'm an asshole."

"Yes. You are. But only to me, and I can take it."

"You shouldn't have to." Wow. It felt surprisingly liberating to say that.

"I understand why you don't respect me. I just wish…" Evan turned his head to stare through the window.

Mike glanced his way and noted the way that Evan's chin had the same dip thing that his had and that their noses both hooked a little to the right. Dylan had the same nose. Mike guessed they all had the same eye color, too. But other than height, there the resemblances ended. "What do you wish?"

Evan was quiet for a while. "That I'd been a little braver when we were kids. Taken a share of the abuse Dylan's sperm donor laid on you. Then you wouldn't have reason to hate me."

Mike rubbed his head. "I don't hate you. I didn't hate you then. I just—"

"I know." Evan cleared his throat. "You know, maybe we should save this true confession business for another time." He gave a short laugh. "Or not. At any rate, you need to slow down. I think we're getting close."

"Okay," Mike said. "Whenever you're ready, though—"

"Uh-huh," Evan said. "Here. Turn here."

Chapter Twenty

Lauren woke with a chemical taste in the back of her throat and a throbbing in her head that felt like someone was beating on the side of her skull. No, it was really someone beating on the side of the cabinet she was resting against.

She looked up and registered who it was trying to wake her. Oh, God. How had she not suspected? "Alex."

Her ex-lover was standing over her and grinning, just as pleased as punch with himself. "Well, there you are. How's your head?"

She was sprawled on the floor of a…lab? In a basement? There were cabinets and counters, shelves of reagent bottles, clean beakers and flasks, graduated cylinders and funnels. A few ancient pieces of lab equipment, an electronic scale, a centrifuge, a hot plate.

"What are you doing? What is all this?"

"What do you think it is?" He pulled an armless computer chair toward himself and straddled it.

"I don't know. Are you—is this your lab?"

He tilted his head, considering. "Duh." He was dressed in his expensively distressed jeans and a long sleeved button-up shirt, but it was wrinkled and sweat stains marred the underarms.

"Are you...are you the one who's been stealing my drugs? What's going on?" She was still foggy from whatever he'd pressed over her face out in the yard, but her sympathetic nervous system was starting to engage, clearing her head and preparing her to react to the danger she was in.

"The thing in Cincinnati didn't work out so well," he said. "I decided that I was better off working on my project under my own supervision."

"Your project?"

"Yes, mine. The one you stole from me."

"What are you talking about?"

"All that help I gave you when we worked together, all those suggestions. Those ideas were mine. The drug is mine."

She wasn't going to argue with him about this right now. Clearly he was delusional or under the influence of some sort of drug. Her drug?

"Alex, have you taken the step two drug yourself?"

Sighing, he ran a hand under his nose. "I had to make sure it was ready for the clinical trial phase of things. You're never going to get it there on your own." He reached into a drawer and pulled out a small vial. A vial that resembled those Lauren used to store step two.

Alex took a pipette from the bench and sucked a few microliters into the tip, then tilted his head back and dropped it into his nose. Pinching his nostrils shut, he looked down at Lauren again. "I've been working out some alternate delivery options for your drug. Of course, I have to deliver it in dried powder form for the junkies. I know you were planning to have it delivered in pill form, but it turns out that this intranasal method works much better. Gets straight to the brain through the olfactory nerve, much quicker."

And much more likely to cause brain damage, Lauren thought. She was fully alert and terrified now. Alex had clearly lost it.

"I figured that you'd get stuck somewhere along the line and need me to bail you out. And I was right. You thought you were having trouble purifying the step two from your algae, didn't you?"

He scratched his arms, the itching a sign that the drug was working. "I know how sensitive you are about doing everything yourself, so at first I was just pinching a little at a time to get you to see that you couldn't make a success of your project without me. And then maybe you'd see that you couldn't make a success of your life without me." He smiled at her in that way he had—he probably thought it was affectionate, but it was really condescending.

"But then I realized that the University of Cincinnati had its ivory tower up its ass"—he flipped his hands around in a *so what* gesture—"so I left there but had to finance my new lab, so I found a market for step two. Which is nice, because this way cuts out the messy FDA approval process. We can make so much more money and not have to answer to institutional bullshit. What do you think?"

He smiled and looked at her, waiting. Was…was he waiting for her to praise him?

"Alex—that's just—" *Crazy. Delusional. Insane…* "That's not the way science is supposed to be done."

His eyelids had fallen to half-mast, and he frowned. The drug he'd dropped into his nose had fully landed in his nervous system. Jerking, he seemed to have processed her comment. "Well, maybe, but I knew you needed me, so I was just speeding things along."

Lauren tried to push herself upright and realized she was bound with duct tape. "Alex, when did you first take step two? I mean, try it as a drug?"

His head snapped up. "When you said we needed a break, I took some with me. I thought that since I wouldn't be there in the lab with you every day, maybe I should do some more experiments with the drug, so that when you realized you still wanted to be with me, I would be ready to help you with your career.

"I did some experiments with it at U.C., but the lab animal people saw that I was using something that wasn't on my protocol, and they closed me down. Assholes. So I tried it on myself."

"Jeez, Alex!"

He swore, then jumped to his feet and began to pace.

Crap. She hadn't meant to set him off, only to try to understand what was going on. She should have let him nod off. She should have stayed home. For that matter, she should have stayed at Mike's house. Why on earth had she thought she didn't want his help? Oh yeah. She remembered now. She wanted his help, she just didn't think she should take it. Some crazy shit about needing to take care of things herself.

"It's good you're here," Alex said. "Your fucking step one pellets aren't working right. I think you left something out of your notes." He motioned at the notebooks stacked on the counter next to her laptop. "You're going to have to show me what secret trick you use to extract the drug."

"I can't do that. I can't let you continue. You're a better person than this!"

He laughed. "I think we're beyond that whole 'You're a misguided good guy' thing. I'm the production department of a big-ass drug distribution operation. And I need to get a shipment to my sales force, so you're going to help me. It's convenient that you showed up, because your lab notes are like reading hieroglyphics, and your lackey hasn't been as helpful as I might have hoped."

"My lackey?" Lauren had a very bad feeling that she knew who Alex meant.

"Dylan, of course." Alex walked across the room to the door to a large storage cabinet. He opened it.

Dylan and his girlfriend were inside, back-to-back, mouths, hands, and feet wrapped with duct tape. They both stared at Lauren, their gazes pleading with her to do something to save them.

She shuddered and fought back against the bile filling her throat. Oh God, this was bad. Very, very bad.

· · ·

Mike parked the truck at the bottom of the drive, out of the line of sight from the house. The lawn had been cut, but no one had pulled any weeds, and the dead foliage from the summer perennials hadn't been cut back or removed. The place looked deserted, except for Lauren's vehicle.

But wait—there was another one almost out of sight behind the house. Was that Alex's? Or—oh, shit—the one that he'd seen Angela Romain driving when she'd dropped

Dylan at Evan's last night.

Next to him, Evan's breath caught in his throat with a barely audible sound. Mike looked at him and knew he was thinking the same thing. Dylan was probably inside, too.

He hoped Dino Romain wasn't on the premises—and said a little prayer that the leader of the Devil's Rangers would take a back seat to this meeting, or whatever it was.

No sense in taking risks, though. He reached behind the seat for his shoulder holster and a jacket to cover the gun he slid into it. Evan watched silently as Mike prepared for battle, leaning out of the way when he took his pistol from the glove box.

"Stay here," Mike told his brother. "If I'm not back in ten minutes, call Crawford."

"Do you really feel that the situation calls for a firearm?" Evan asked.

"I'm a cop, even if I am on suspension. I'm qualified to know when to use it," Mike said. And for the first time in a long time, he believed it. He *was* qualified. Not only to use the firearm—he'd never doubted his aim—but to defend someone he loved.

"I'm coming with you," Evan sounded nervous, but there was a light in his eyes that Mike recognized as determination.

Mike looked at his brother, tempted to hug him, but was afraid the ground might open up beneath their feet to swallow them whole if he did—and he wouldn't be able to help Lauren if that happened.

Would she even want his help? Well, fuck it. She was going to get it. She could hate him later, and that was fine. This had gone beyond just getting his job and reputation back and wanting to stop the people who set him up and ruined

Dylan's life. This was about giving the woman he loved the opportunity to do everything with her life that she aspired to. Didn't matter what happened to him—he wasn't going to see Lauren suffer.

Careful not to make a sound on the gravel driveway, they made their way the couple of hundred yards to the property edge, then detoured through the woods when they got close to the house. Edging through the trees, they made their way around to the back. The door to a walkout basement was opened a few inches.

"If we can get over there," Mike said, pointing to a tall stand of elephant grass that was falling over next to the southwest corner, "I think we can check things out without being in view of any of the windows."

"What, exactly, are we going to do when we get there?" Evan asked.

"See where everyone is, what's going on, and then get everyone out of there in one piece."

"Good. That's good. Gather information, build a hypothesis. But the 'getting everyone out in one piece' part. How does that happen?"

"One step at a time." He wished he were as certain as his words suggested that everything would be okay.

"All right." The trust that Evan was putting in Mike helped push his own self-doubt further out of his own line of sight. This was good, he needed to focus.

Mike paused and looked at Evan. No longer pale, his brother's cheeks were flushed. "Dude, you okay?"

"I'm torn between paralyzed with fear and ready to dive through a window without protective gear."

Mike nodded. "Okay, then. You're fine. Let's go see what

we can find out."

• • •

Lauren's stomach lurched and she fought to keep from puking. How had someone like Alex—a man with a brilliant mind—come to this? Good God, the man had *kidnapped* Dylan and his girlfriend!

Was it about the money? She didn't think so. His family was pretty well-off and had always seemed supportive, if a little...helicopter-ish.

Maybe that was why Alex had felt the need to be over-the-top involved in Lauren's work. Maybe he was the second coming of Norman Bates and was working out his mommy issues with her.

Why hadn't Lauren realized how messed up he was? How had she allowed her own fears about losing control of her own life blind herself to the fact that there were just some people out there who needed to take over other people's lives? Alex was one of those people. Mike was not.

Lauren was suddenly very pissed off, which wasn't helping things any, but at least the nausea had receded.

"I'm going to set something up here," Alex told Lauren. "And then you're going to tell me, step-by-step, how to harvest step two from this ridiculous algae."

He looked pointedly at the bag of pellets sitting on the counter, and then back at her. "And if you don't do it right, I'll know, because I'm going to test it on him." He nodded at Dylan, who was wiggling his jaw in an attempt to loosen the duct tape covering his mouth. "My own human test monkey."

Alex walked to the shelf of glass beakers. Within seconds, he'd mixed chemicals from the flammables cabinet and the one marked "organic acids," and then added something from a white plastic jar. None of these chemicals were part of her research protocol.

Lauren thought, somewhat hysterically, that it was a good thing that he'd clearly marked his chemical storage, because when the occupational safety inspectors came, he wouldn't get any nasty notes about dangerous conditions. Her vision tunneled, and she fought against the rising panic. She needed to think. To figure out how to get her and Dylan out of this mess. But how?

Alex always liked to be the educator. Maybe if she got him to talk, he would get distracted and—what exactly? "What are you doing?" she asked.

"I'm making a booby trap. Or maybe I should call it a 'Bobby' trap." He laughed. "See what I did there? I made a pun. Because your so-called maintenance man, the guy you're screwing? He's really an impotent has-been cop. Kind of like a London Bobby—they're still forbidden from carrying guns, aren't they?" He shrugged. "No matter. You get the irony, right?"

"Alex, this is—" She stopped herself before she said "crazy." Even though it was. He seemed to be a little on the sensitive side right now. "This isn't necessary. I can tell you what you need to know about getting from step one to step two. Let Dylan and Angela go, okay?"

"Nope. I think everyone's going to stay right here for now." Alex carried a set of beakers, nested in one another, each filled with something, over to the door. He set the beaker down just out of sight of the slightly open back door.

Anyone who came in would kick it over. Brushing off his hands, he straightened and went back to the bench. "There. Now, if anyone tries to interrupt us before our work is done, they'll get blown up." He looked at Lauren. "Hopefully, it won't blow you up, too."

Lauren thought about Evan, who might—this very moment—be on his way here to help her try to talk to Dylan. Would he burst in here, trying to save the day, and trigger the homemade bomb? Would he have called Mike and brought him? She'd asked him not to, but... It occurred to her that instead of helping this family, she might have single-handedly just managed to kill them all. The urge to empty her stomach all over the floor returned with a vengeance, and she had to take deep breaths to stay in control.

Alex continued to putter about the lab bench, mixing things together. When he had all of his booby traps set up, he put the bag of algae pellets on the counter.

"Now, Dr. Kane, let's talk about step two production. AKA Methyl-oxy-morphicol. AKA Devil's Dust."

Lauren prayed. She prayed that somehow, Dylan and Angela would escape. She prayed that if she didn't survive this, if all that the police found was her burned, smoking corpse, there would be enough evidence left to yield the proof that Mike needed to put Alex away for a long, long time. And she prayed that, if for some reason she managed to survive, Mike would listen when she apologized for walking out on him.

• • •

Mike checked behind him to see that Evan was okay as they

reached the back of the house and crept to the open door.

He heaved a silent sigh of relief when Lauren's voice drifted through the open door. "Come on, Alex," he could hear her say. "I'll stay and do whatever you want, but please. You've got to let Dylan and Angela go. They don't have anything to do with this."

Oh, God. His tension immediately rose as he registered the words. He looked at Evan, then at the door hiding Dylan and Lauren from view. Everyone he cared for was right here, and they all needed him to keep them safe. He hoped he wasn't about to fuck it up.

"You're not going to do anything stupid, are you?" Evan asked in a voice quieter than a whisper, perfected many years ago to avoid the wrath of a drunken stepfather.

"Define stupid."

"Try to go in there alone and get killed."

He certainly wasn't planning to take Evan in with him. And he didn't *want* to die, but he would if it meant his family—and that included Lauren now, and even Angela, since she was important to Dylan—would survive.

What he needed was a distraction to pull Alex out of the basement so that he could get in there and free his family.

The sound of a car pulling into the driveway met Mike's ears. A door opened, then another. Then feet, doors slamming, and the telltale crackle and squawk of a police radio. Perfect. He grinned. "The cavalry has arrived."

They exchanged a silent fist bump and waited for Crawford and his men to draw Alex out of the basement.

• • •

"Alex, did you do all that damage to my lab yourself?" Lauren asked, trying to keep her voice steady, to keep Alex talking. Could she manage to get through to him on an intellectual level? Or was she just stalling the inevitable? Stalling was good. It might give her a chance to think of some way to get free.

Alex looked at her. "I brought a friend."

"Was that who drew the graffiti on the wall?"

He laughed. "That was brilliant, I think. I knew your little buddy here had been in trouble with the Rangers—that's how I got in contact with them in the first place. I heard him whining to Evan Adams about wanting to see his *girlfriend*." He walked over to Dylan and patted him on the head. "Evan actually thought that the little girlfriend could put Dylan's probation at risk because of her affiliation with that 'drug gang.'" He mimicked Evan's formal speech pattern. "Adams is such a pansy. But after I had acquired enough of your step two to fund my little research and development program here, knowing about the Rangers did give me an idea for distribution. I took them some samples, they liked them, and I promised them more. Except you did something to the algae, didn't you?"

The sound of the doorbell echoed through the house.

Alex said, "What the hell?"

Lauren was about to shout for help when Alex stepped next to a beaker that was perilously close to Dylan's bound feet. "Ah, ah!" he admonished. He tore a strip of duct tape from the roll and plastered it to Lauren's face, covering her mouth, then picked up the beaker and set it between her knees. "There. If you drop that, we'll all go up in smoke. Hold tight, I'll be back in a few."

She glanced at Dylan, who looked concerned but not panicked. And Angela looked only mildly panicked. That was good. They all needed to keep a cool head. Or something. She really didn't know what they needed. Besides Mike.

Alex shut the door on the cabinet, hiding Dylan and Angela from view, then jogged up the stairs and out of sight.

"Hello, officers. How can I help you?" Alex's voice carried to the basement through a cold air return in the floor.

The police. Thank God. Lauren tried to smile reassuringly at Dylan and Angela.

"Are you Alex Barker?" A smooth, deep voice that Lauren recognized as Chief Crawford's went a long way toward reassuring herself. "We've received a report of some unusual activity in this neighborhood."

"Glad you're here," Alex said, his voice carrying down the stairs. "I was about to call you. I've been in Cincinnati for the past few months, but when I came in, I had the distinct feeling that something was wrong here."

"Can you tell us what that is?"

"Well, I'm not sure. I mean, I'm afraid…" Alex paused. "Okay, I hate to—well, it's my girlfriend. Dr. Lauren Kane."

Lauren jerked then, nearly dislodging the beaker between her knees. She wasn't worried about losing it, she'd always won the walk-with-an orange-between-your-legs contests at birthday parties. But the other beakers inside were floating rather precariously.

"Dr. Kane, from Tucker University, is your girlfriend?" Crawford's voice was tinged with only a hint of disbelief.

"Well, we dated for a while, and she's been—well, she's been asking me to reconcile with her. That's her car, right there."

"Is she here?"

"No, that's the problem. I'm very concerned. I'm worried that she's into something bad for her."

"And what would that be?"

"The drug that she makes in her lab. I'm sure you've heard about the vandalism at Tuck U?"

There was a sound of affirmation from upstairs.

"I'm pretty sure that she's been selling one of her drug products to a gang in Cincinnati."

"Is that so?"

Oh, hell, Lauren thought. Was he going to set her up? That asshat. It crossed her mind that any more suspicion of her integrity would wreck any chance she had of getting support from the Pemberton group, but at this point, she was more concerned with her life than her career.

Alex's voice continued, but so soft now she had trouble making him out. She thought she heard something about Alex allowing Lauren to stay here in this house but that she hadn't been responding to his messages asking her to return his key.

A noise on the other side of the room had her jerking her head around, nearly upsetting the beakers she held. *Mike.* Large, in charge, and fired up. Her heart flipped into overdrive. With her eyes, she tried to warn him, but as he pushed the sliding door open, his big foot knocked over the beaker Alex had set there.

There was a slight hissing sound and then a whoosh as flames shot across the floor, following the path of the spilled liquid.

"Shit." He came in, pulling a knife from his belt. He cut

the bindings on her hands and then her feet.

She put the beaker she held down on the floor, then pulled the duct tape from her mouth.

"We need to get out of here," she said. But when she stood up, she didn't take into account that her feet had gone to sleep from the lack of circulation. She stumbled…right into the beaker she'd just put on the floor. It caught fire, just like the one by the door, except the burning alcohol in this container ran straight toward the flammable cabinet. Which was next to the one holding Dylan and Angela captive.

"In there!" she told Mike.

He crossed the room and opened the door, then quickly cut through Dylan's bindings while Lauren fumbled with Angela's. Her fingers were next to useless, though, and ac- rid smoke from the makeshift booby traps began to choke her. Mike tugged her out of the way and took care of free- ing the girl. "Let's go!" Mike shouted, grabbing her arm and shoving Dylan out ahead of him. Dylan, in turn, had his arm around Angela and was supporting her.

Lauren started to go along, and then, at the last second, jerked away. "Wait! I need to get something!"

"Fuck, Lauren, leave it!" Mike shouted at her.

She looked at him for a split second that lasted a lifetime, then turned and grabbed the bag of algae pellets on the counter. And hoped he'd listen to her explanation later. If there was a later.

Chapter Twenty-One

Mike watched as Lauren—God*damn* it—risked her fucking neck to grab a handful of vials and the bag of that fucking algae, which she proceeded to stuff into the pocket of her hoodie.

With no time to be gentle, he put a firm hand around her arm and pushed her ahead of him toward the door—but the flames blocked their path. As he hesitated, he heard a hiss and a popping sound from the other side of the room.

"Oh, God. It's going to blow up," Lauren said. "I'm so sorry."

He looked down at her. It no longer mattered that she was endangering them both to save her career by going back for that fucking algae. It didn't matter that his own hopes for redemption were going up in smoke—and into Lauren's pocket—he wasn't going to let this woman die.

"Let it," he said, and then he kissed her. It was a hard, fast kiss, but he tried to put everything he had into it. If he failed, he wanted her last memory of him to be of how much she meant to him. But it wouldn't be her last memory. Not if he had anything to do with it.

He bent, hoisted her over his shoulder, and ran through the smoke and flames to fresh air and freedom.

They shot into the backyard, following Dylan and Angela away from the house. He put Lauren back on her feet. "Let's go," he said, and grabbed her hand to pull her along with him. They'd talk about the kiss later. About how much he wanted her. Needed her. Didn't deserve her. Right now he had to make damned sure they were out of the line of fire — because that house was going to blow.

Evan was ahead of them, running toward the woods after the retreating figure of Alex Barker. Then, as Crawford yelled from the side of the house, Evan turned slightly, and the world went into slow-mo.

Mike later couldn't remember what he heard first, the explosion behind him as the lab blew up or the crack of a bullet firing from a pistol somewhere ahead of him. He held Lauren's hand tighter, pulling her closer to shield her with his body, as he watched Evan collapse.

And then there was a long, low, hoarse shout. "Evaaaaaaan!"

He only realized the sound had come from his own throat moments later, when Lauren gripped his bicep and said, "I'm safe — go to him!" He let her go and ran to his brother, who was writhing in the weeds.

Evan grabbed Mike's arm and pointed, "He went that way!"

"Jesus, fuck. Oh my God. Don't you die, you asshole," Mike said, checking Evan for a pulse, even though he realized that was stupid, that if Evan was talking to him, his heart was probably still beating. But he'd been shot. There was blood on his leg—

Crawford was there and pulled at his arm. "Mike, let me see. Back up." Mike shook him off, and then Dylan was on Mike's other side, also trying to talk to him—but all he could see through his panicked haze was Evan, bleeding and in pain.

Until Lauren wrapped her arm around his back, her familiar scent filling his head and bringing calm reason with her. He looked up, and her wobbly smile told him that it was okay. Right now, at least, it was okay. Next to her, Dylan squatted, concern—but not fear—creasing his forehead.

He stood, rising on shaking legs.

Finally, he managed to back up enough so Crawford could bend over Evan, to see that there was a hole just below the pocket of his jeans, a hole that was leaking darkly, soaking into the denim.

Through gritted teeth, Evan ground out, "That fuckbrain shot me in the ass. Find him and string him up."

Lauren smiled tightly as she took the T-shirt Dylan pulled off his own back, wadded it up, then pressed it against Evan's backside, which caused him to send out another colorful string of curses.

"Dude," Dylan said. "I didn't know you even knew words like that."

"I know a lot of words I choose not to use," Evan said, groaning as Mike shifted his hand a little with the makeshift bandage.

"What were you trying to do?" Mike asked.

"Trying to catch him," Evan gasped. "I saw the smoke

from downstairs, then he came running around the side of the house."

Mike saw Crawford shrug. "We weren't expecting the place to blow up," he said.

The cop who'd headed into the woods after Alex, was back, bent over, breathing hard, gasping. "He." *Gasp.* "Got." *Gasp.* "Away." *Gasp. Choke.*

Over his shoulder, Mike felt a wave of heat as another explosion rent the morning. Regret, dismay, and self-recrimination washed over him. He'd done this—he'd let Dylan endanger himself, and done one worse and gotten Evan shot. Once again, he hadn't been able to take care of his siblings the way he'd promised their grandmother. The way he'd promised himself.

"Dispatch," Crawford said into his radio. "Send a 'hurry up' to that fire truck and the ambulance, would you?" He turned to Lauren. "What was that nutcase doing in there?"

"He stole my drug. Alex did. He's the one. He was trying to purify it and was selling it to those Devil's Rangers people, but he didn't know what he was doing. And he was using it."

A siren wailed in the distance, growing closer, but not fast enough.

"Evan, I'm so sorry I dragged you out here," Mike said. He couldn't even look at Dylan. As soon as they got home, as soon as Evan was okay, Mike was going to make Dylan move in with Evan and get himself as far away from the both of them as possible.

Evan could anal-retentive their younger brother to death, but Dylan would still be better off without Mike's fucked up supervision.

And as for Lauren, well, she could keep her algae pellets

and her step two drug, take them to the Pemberton Group and make her pitch, do whatever she needed to do. He wouldn't stand in her way.

He was done looking for redemption at any cost. That had been a load of self-centered bullshit, anyway. All he wanted was to keep Lauren, Dylan, and Evan safe. He'd find Alex Barker and bring him to justice, one way or another.

• • •

Lauren waited in the interview room of the Tucker Police Department. It was as far from the dirty green-painted cinderblock interview rooms she'd seen on cop shows as could be. Instead, a dark wood conference table was surrounded by comfortable chairs. A single-cup coffee maker in the corner had supplied her with a cup of now-cold amaretto-flavored brew to fiddle with while she waited for Crawford to tell her that she could leave.

Fatigue swamped her, the events of the day a biochemical black hole, sucking the energy from her cells. She closed her eyes and dropped her head into her hand, but the video screen in her brain played images of Mike's cold profile as he'd turned away from her when he and Dylan got into the back of the ambulance with Evan.

She'd really screwed up with Mike. Her pride, her stupid knee-jerk need for independence had driven her to run out on him—was it only this morning? And all that shit with Alex had happened since then, in a few short hours—and now there was really no need for Mike to see her again. It was all over.

Well, that was fine. She tried to tell herself that she didn't need to be with someone who could brush her off that easily. Better to know now than invest her heart and soul in the relationship. At least she hadn't wasted too much time. Or been through any messy holidays or birthdays with gifts that might sit on that fuzzy "Should I return this?" line. Or gotten an "I love Mike Gibson" tattoo on her butt.

She must have drifted off, because she was jolted awake when the door finally opened to admit Chief Crawford. His face was drawn with exhaustion. She guessed hers didn't look much better.

"I'm sorry to keep you waiting," he said. "We had three sorority girls admitted to the hospital for alcohol poisoning this morning, on top of the mess with Barker."

"Did you find him?" she asked.

"No, I'm sorry. We've got an APB out for him, but he hasn't been spotted. We've also had dogs trying to pick up his scent, but apparently, he found a car to steal at a neighbor's farm, and they lost him."

"What about Evan?" she asked. What she really wanted to know was if Crawford had seen Mike, but she didn't ask.

"Evan's going to be okay. He had surgery to remove the bullet, and they're keeping him overnight to watch for signs of infection, but he should be released in the morning. You can go see him if you want after this."

Lauren nodded. "What about the algae I gave you? And the drug in the vials? Are you going to be able to use that to make a case against Alex?"

"We could, if we find Alex. And...I put in a call to Mike's old boss and told him everything that happened."

"And? Is he going to reinstate Mike?"

Crawford shook his head. "They're glad to have Devil's

Dust off the street, don't get me wrong. But unless they can get proof that your boy Alex was selling the shit to the Rangers? They can't get Dino Romain, and that's what Mike's job hinges on."

And they couldn't get Dino if they didn't have Alex.

God only knew where Alex was or if he'd ever get caught.

In a moment of what she knew was pure selfish resentment, she wished she hadn't turned over the evidence. If it wasn't going to matter anyway, she could have used it to make enough step three to take to the Pemberton Group.

"Thank you." She had to ask, "How long will you have to keep that algae I gave you?" When she'd turned the algae in to Crawford, she had to tell him why she'd left that out of her original inventory of what was missing from her lab. That she needed it to keep her project moving.

Crawford hadn't accused her of withholding evidence, had only blinked and put it with the couple of milliliters of step two that remained in the vial she'd taken from the basement lab.

Now he said, "I'm sorry. It will be a long, long time. I know you needed it to make enough drug for your research project. I'm sorry that I can't return it to you before your meeting."

Lauren shrugged. Like it was no big deal.

She realized—with a hollowness blooming in her gut—that losing Mike was the big crater in the middle of her life. The end of her career was the muck at the bottom, but she had a feeling she'd be stuck in that hole whether she had a job to return to or not.

"Well, you did the right thing," Crawford told her. "Mike's a good man. And he's lucky to have you in his camp."

"Yeah, I'm not sure he sees it that way," Lauren murmured.

• • •

"Thanks for stopping by," Mike told the old guy, Dr. Jerrold, as he left Evan's hospital room. What he really wanted to say was "You've got your head completely up your ass," but he held back.

The fucker had told Mike that there was no way Lauren would be able to get her funding back and her suspension lifted before the meeting later in the week—even if she could get enough of her drug made in time—and she should be able to do that, since she'd grabbed up that algae from the lab. Apparently, the Pemberton board of directors had decided that it was too risky to back a project that had garnered so much notoriety.

Mike had completely and utterly failed her. And once again, let someone get away from a crime scene with a boatload of drugs. Granted, the situation was completely different this time. Unlike when Dino Romain had made off with all of that heroin, Lauren wasn't going to turn her haul into little packets of death for drug addicts—and Mike wouldn't go back and change things, he wouldn't try to stop her from pocketing the algae and shit, but...it just hadn't made any difference.

The incessant beeping of the monitors attached to Evan was a challenge to Mike's tenuous hold on sanity. Every now and then, Evan would thrash his arms around and an alarm would go off, requiring a nurse to stroll in, push a button, and wander back out.

In spite of the occasional momentary nightmare, Evan seemed comfortable. The morphine pump was probably helping. Mike wondered briefly if Lauren's drug would ever be used in this sort of a situation.

Jesus. What an exercise in futility this had all been. He needed the Devil's Dust shit in evidence to link Alex to Dino and get his job back—though without Alex, the drug didn't help Mike—and Lauren needed the same thing in her lab to get her job back—and she had it—but without funding from those Pemberton assholes, it was too late.

Evan moaned, then settled back into drugged oblivion.

Mike was on a roll. He'd gotten one brother shot, and alienated the other. He'd refused to believe that Dylan could be trying to do the right thing, had never even given the kid a chance to let him into what was going on in that big heart of his.

The fact was, Dylan was just a man in love. Not the woman Mike would have chosen for him, but love-life regulation clearly wasn't under Mike's jurisdiction. Hell, he couldn't stop Dylan from falling in love—he couldn't even stop himself.

Dylan came in with two cups of coffee and a bag of powdered donuts. "Dude, why don't you go on home? Get some sleep. I'll stay here tonight."

"No. You can go, though. I'll stretch out on that." Mike pointed to the vinyl couch thing that sat under a window.

"I slept all afternoon. When did you sleep?"

"It doesn't matter. I'm good. Where's Angela?" And why was the kid even talking to him?

Dylan sighed and dropped into a chair. "She went home." He propped his enormous Converse sneakers on the end of Evan's bed and dug into the donuts. "Go. Go home."

"I'm good."

"Well, I'm staying," Dylan said, spraying powdered sugar over his black T-shirt. "We could sit here and have a martyr contest, but you've already earned that badge. I can't beat you."

"What the fuck are you talking about?"

"You're better at throwing yourself on swords than the rest of us."

"Huh?"

"I mean throwing your job away to try to save me."

Shit. He never wanted Dylan to carry that weight. It was Mike's, and only Mike's. "I'm supposed to take care of you."

Dylan got up and walked across the room, stopping at the doorway and holding up his hand in a stop gesture to someone outside of Mike's line of sight. "You've done that. You've given me a place to live. You've helped me get into school. When I got in trouble last year, you threw yourself under the bus for me. Maybe it's time for me to grow up a little."

That was bullshit. Dylan had been forced to grow up way too soon. Mike felt pressure that he'd been holding in for ten years press against the backs of his eyes. "Don't you remember how I almost killed you?"

"What? What are you talking about?"

Mike walked over to his brother and pulled the kid's T-shirt up, exposing the scarring that marred what should have been a smooth, pale stomach. "I left you alone. I'm responsible for this."

He turned away, unable to bear the blame he knew he'd see on Dylan's face. He spun and looked straight into the shocked eyes of Lauren, who stood in the hall, listening to everything. He saw her lips, her perfect lips, form the word, "What…?"

He held her gaze. Let her hear it from the horse's ass. "I left him alone. I was supposed to be watching him. I was in the backyard, trying to get into Allie Dunham's pants. Dylan was hungry."

Dylan made a sound of disbelief. "I was eight years old, Mike, not four! I knew I wasn't supposed to be cooking. I made the decision. I wasn't starving, and there was peanut butter and jelly. I remember, because that's what you laid out for me on the counter. I'm the one who decided I needed a hamburger and started the damned grease fire."

Lauren held his gaze, but she flinched at Dylan's words.

Mike blinked first. He picked up his jacket and walked out, brushing past Lauren.

"Mike?" She caught his arm before made it into the stairwell.

"This isn't a good time," he said.

She held on to his arm, and finally, he looked at her.

She stood there, looking at him so…hopefully?

God. She was so fucking beautiful, wearing stiff, cheap jeans, sneakers, and that old Tucker University sweatshirt, her hair in a ponytail, no makeup, just…her.

She said, "I just wanted to say—I'm sorry about this morning, or—that was this morning, wasn't it?" She shook her head, smiling ruefully. "Wow, huh?"

He was pretty sure that if he tried to pull her into his arms, she'd let him, but if he did that—he'd never let her go.

And she needed someone who didn't ruin everything he touched. Not only had he not gotten her algae back in time, but he hadn't stopped the bastard who had hurt her.

"So, Evan's okay?" she asked. "That's what—Chief Crawford told me a little while ago."

"Yeah, he's gonna be pretty miserable for a while, but as long as the antibiotics work, and he takes it easy…"

"Good. That's good."

She was still looking at him, he guessed expecting something, but he couldn't—

She put her arms around his waist and leaned into him. "I'm glad you're okay, too." The weight of her body pressed against him, holding him together for just a few more minutes, delaying the inevitable shattering of his heart.

Shit. He wanted to return the gesture, but after that scene with Dylan, after everything she'd heard, how did she think…

He unwound her arms and pushed her gently away. "I can't do this," he said and stepped around her, shoving the door open and running down the stairs and out into the cold night air.

Chapter Twenty-Two

Mike let himself into the maintenance office, relieved that no one was there. He'd been to the campus gym, beaten the hell out of the heavy bag, and scared the shit out of a couple of frat boys who were pretending to train for some all-Greek MMA thing. Mike wondered if their parents knew that their tuition money was funding head injuries and broken collarbones but decided he didn't really care.

All he was trying to do was make himself tired enough to sleep. He didn't know what else to do. There was always bourbon, but he played that tape in his mind and it ended with him waking up in a puddle of vomit on the bathroom floor.

He just kept hearing Dylan's words, over and over in his head. "There was peanut butter and jelly." Was it that simple? Had the tragic accident that scarred his little brother, earned Mike a beating, and ultimately estranged him from Evan, all been just a freak *thing*?

Maybe. Maybe if Dylan had listened to Mike and made a damned sandwich instead of lighting a fire under a grease-filled skillet, maybe if Evan hadn't been at the library, hiding from Dylan's psycho, drug addict father, maybe if Mike hadn't been so focused on getting into Allie Dunham's panties… But there were three legs to that table. And Mike was one of them. If he'd been there, Dylan wouldn't have been hurt.

The door to the office creaked open and Jason came in.

"What are you doing here?" Mike asked. "It's a little past your bedtime, isn't it?"

"Crawford called me. Said security got a call from the Rec Center about some crazy asshole trying to kill either himself or a punching bag." The older man sat down on the bench next to Mike. "You wanna tell me what the hell your problem is?"

"Not really." Mike tore off his sweaty T-shirt and wiped his underarms with it before taking a new one from his locker and pulling it over his head.

"I hear Evan's going to be okay."

"Yeah. He was in surgery for a while, they had to dig around a bit to get the bullet out. He'll be in there for a day or so, getting pumped full of antibiotics, but he'll make it."

"That's good. He's an odd bird, but he's a decent guy."

Mike sighed. "Yeah. He is. I—I haven't given him a fair shake."

Jason rubbed his head, looking at the floor. "Yeah, I know. But you didn't get much in the way of support yourself. I should have stepped up after Lloyd died and been a father figure or something like that, but I suck at this emotional shit. Hell, I can't even admit that I'm afraid I'm not good enough to work for my wife's family, so I hide out here with my tool belt. They keep asking, though."

"What do they want you to do for them?" Mike asked.

Jason chuckled. "Miss Emmaline wants me to evaluate the requirements for those crazy grants that she offers faculty members. She says I'm in a unique position to be objective about the projects and to have a 'plumber's eye view'— her words, not mine—of the people who are applying. She says I probably know more about the personal integrity of everyone on campus."

"You probably do," Mike told him. "You should give it a shot."

Jason harrumphed.

It was silent then, except for the buzzing of a fluorescent light fixture that needed to be replaced.

Mike thought about everything that had happened over the last few days, weeks, years. He thought about the anger that he carried around with him, the blame, the constant fear. It was all about fear, wasn't it?

And what was he afraid of? That he would fail to protect his family? And what did that mean? That they would leave him? Keeping everyone at arm's length, what did that accomplish? Not a goddamned thing.

Jason swore. "See? I'm lousy father material. I came in here to make you feel better about whatever was bothering you, and instead, I just pile my own shit on your sandwich."

Mike laughed. This time it felt more real. "But you're so good at being an inappropriate uncle."

Then something occurred to him. "Jason, you definitely need to take Miss Emmaline up on her job offer. I know the perfect person to receive one of her grants."

...

Lauren sighed and tried to make herself comfortable, sitting on a too-hard mattress, leaning against too-soft pillows, in a too-empty room at the Tuck U Inn. Because she didn't want to think about anything else, she tried to mentally plan the next day. At least maybe she'd hear from Dr. Jerrold that she'd be allowed back on campus, since she couldn't go home until a professional cleaning service had been through to remove the traces of Dylan's cologne—his former cologne, he'd promised her—that Alex had spread around the house to throw suspicion off of himself. Okay, so much for not thinking about Alex, or Devil's Dust, or…Mike.

Lauren flipped—twice—through all of the channels so kindly provided by the Tuck U Inn for her viewing pleasure, but each time she got to the end of the list, she realized she hadn't registered any of the choices. She thought about going for a third spin around the TV dial, just to give her hands something to do besides pick at her cuticles, but she felt the need to check her phone for non-existent messages first. Nope. None. But then again, what had she expected?

No matter how many times she tried to focus on something else, her mind kept turning back to that run-in with Mike at the hospital. He had looked at her with something akin to disappointment, almost disgust. God, she was such a fool. She'd really thought that they had something going. Something beyond a couple of earth-shattering orgasms each. But clearly she'd overstepped her bounds by showing up at the hospital tonight.

After Mike pulled his disappearing act, Lauren had

slunk in to see Evan and talk to Dylan, who tried valiantly to act like nothing was wrong, that he hadn't just been having it out with his oldest brother.

Evan had woken up for a few minutes and asked Lauren to feed his frogs while he was out of commission. She suppressed her usual grin as she said she'd feed the little FU-CRs. Then he wanted her to move the monitor with his vital statistics so that he could see it and *then,* he wanted her to tell him how much, and what color, the urine draining into the bag at the foot of the bed was. Finally, he pushed the button on his morphine pump and drifted back to la-la land.

Dylan told her about Angela, about how, even though they knew that both of their families disapproved, she'd called him a few months ago. Dylan had told her that he couldn't see her because of the crap that Dino had gotten him into, and she'd shocked him with a suggestion that they try to nail Dino for his drug dealing. Angela couldn't bear to see any more of her friends carted off in caskets or handcuffs.

So they'd been hanging around, following Dino whenever possible, until a few days ago, when Angela had come to Dylan and told him she thought, based on something she'd overheard, that her brother had something to do with the Devil's Dust situation. And that was why they'd been hanging around in front of Lauren's house. Hoping to catch Dino breaking in. Unfortunately, they'd caught Alex Barker, instead. Or rather, he'd caught them, trying to catch him. That was how they'd wound up in a closet in his basement.

She and Dylan had then shared a little more small talk, ignoring any and all elephants that had taken up residence in the hospital room, and then Lauren had officially had enough of the Gibson-Adams-White family for one day.

She'd headed for the Tuck U Inn, where she made friends with the clerk at the front desk—she recognized him from a class she'd taught last spring but couldn't remember his name. Looked like a science major wasn't doing him much good.

Huh. Wasn't doing her much good, either.

The phone rang, yanking her out of her self-pity spin cycle and into the "Is it gonna be Mike?" agitator.

Nope.

"Hi, Mom."

"Talk to me," Karen Kane demanded. "I got your message—and understood most of it, even through the sniffling. I don't think that getting that drug off the street and finding out Alex was responsible is why you were crying, though."

Of course not, but how did she say this? Better to just yank off the Band-Aid. "Mom, I'm sorry. I messed up, and I don't think I can be a scientist anymore."

"Huh? I thought this was going to be about the guy. What was his name?"

"Mike. And yeah, there's probably a little of that, too." *A little* being more than half, but as far as her mom was concerned...

"Wait," her mom said. "Please don't tell me you've been pursuing a career in science because you think you owe it to me?"

Lauren thought about it for a minute. "No. I love science. This is what I want to do. But I didn't think I could have a family and a successful job at the same time."

"I'm so sorry."

"Don't be. I've finally realized that I can have as much as I'm willing to let myself have." And it was true.

Unfortunately, she'd realized this a little too late to have it with the one man she wanted.

After hanging up with her mom, she decided to walk to one of the fast food restaurants across the street. She thought about splurging on a Big Mac, large fries, and a large chocolate shake, but that seemed too much like wallowing. When she got to the counter, she ordered a salad. With extra ranch dressing. And large fries. And a large chocolate shake.

Back at the Tuck U Inn, the clerk from the front desk was standing outside, pretending not to smoke a cigarette. Or maybe a joint. At least she knew it wasn't her algae—she'd checked the bag she'd taken from Alex's lab, and it was almost all there. Whatever he'd taken out to sell to his test subjects had already gone up in flames.

The clerk—what *was* his name?—smiled at her. "There you are. I thought you were still in your room. Your boyfriend just went up to see you."

"Boyfriend?" The kid had to be mistaken.

"Yeah, some good-looking dude. Seemed kinda crazy about you. I didn't tell him what room you were in, but I did pull up your info on the computer to ring your room, and he kinda leaned over the counter and saw your room number. Took off running toward your room. The dude definitely is crushing on you."

Mike was here? Hope flooded her chest and she almost dropped her milkshake. "Thanks!" She practically ran up the outdoor stairs to the second-floor balcony, going over what she would say in her mind as she took the steps. "I can't live without you" seemed a little desperate, considering how he'd pushed her away earlier. Would "Why are you here?" be too cold? Before she'd decided, she was there. She came around the corner, and stopped. There was no one standing outside her room.

Disappointment replaced the hope that had bloomed in her chest just a few seconds before. Had Mike changed his mind and left?

She slowly walked the rest of the way to her room, shivering as an evening breeze wafted over her. After sliding her key card through the slot and shoving the door open, she made it across the threshold before she realized the room wasn't empty.

Alex Barker sat in the middle of her bed, a handgun pointed straight at her heart. A big—very big—black gun. "Come on in, sweetheart. Thanks for bringing me dinner."

Lauren froze.

"Close the door."

She pushed the door behind her and heard it click shut on her life. "What do you want?"

"Well, let's start with dinner. I haven't eaten in…" He looked at the ceiling. "A couple of days." It didn't appear that he'd showered in at least as long. He was still wearing the same rumpled clothes he'd had on that morning.

Fear and anger let pity look in, but then shoved it away. "Alex, what are you doing? Why did you do this to yourself?"

He sighed. "I'm not going to go back through the list of the ways you could have avoided this. Let's just move on to what's going to happen next."

"Okay…"

"After I eat your dinner, we're going to leave here. We're going to go to the lab and get the algae that you have growing and take it somewhere far from here."

He gestured to her to hand him the bag of food. She did,

and he looked inside, not releasing the pistol, and cursed. "A salad? Christ. That's not going to cut it."

There was a knock at the door. Lauren's heart stuttered.

Alex was on his feet in an instant, behind the door, gun aimed at Lauren. "Get rid of them."

She peered through the peephole. Oh, God. *Mike*. She'd hoped he would come, but now that he was here, fear for him roiled through her. She had to keep him safe—even if it meant breaking her own heart.

Chapter Twenty-Three

Mike's pulse beat hard and fast as he stared at Lauren's frowning face. He'd have a hell of a lot of groveling to do to get her to smile again, he figured. "I'm an asshole," he said, holding up a bouquet of daisies.

She didn't take it from him, so he lowered it to his side.

"Yeah. So?" Lauren leaned on the edge of the open door, not opening it far enough to admit him.

Damn. He was too late. There was no way she was going to give him a chance now. What did he expect? "Look, can I come in? It's chilly out here."

"You should have put on a jacket." Her lips were pursed, a sure sign of a disgusted woman, but her upper chest and neck were flushed and she didn't quite meet his gaze.

Mike cleared his throat. "I, um…I haven't handled much of anything well today." That was an understatement. "As a matter of fact, I haven't handled anything well in—hell, my whole fucking life."

"Okay," she said, pale and shaky. "I don't really want to talk to you right now."

"All right, then. I probably should stick with the program and not handle this well, either, so I'll just do it right here on the second floor balcony of the Tuck U Inn."

She glanced to the side, then said, "Really, Mike, not now."

"Just one minute, then I'll go, okay?"

Her eyes were almost…pleading? He needed to make this fast.

"I've spent the past ten years trying to make up for shit that maybe other people should have been responsible for, and trying to fix things that couldn't be fixed. If Dr. Phil was here, he'd probably tell me I have trust and control issues."

She'd raised an eyebrow and was looking at him now. "You don't say."

"I let that bleed into our relationship."

"We have — had — a relationship?" She had wedged most of her body into the six inches that the door was opened.

Mike swallowed. He looked away, over the parking area below. "I think so. I'm not so sure I'd know what that — a relationship — looks like, but if it's me wanting to be around you constantly, thinking about you when I'm not, and when freaky shit happens, my first instinct is to come find you, then I think, at least on my end, that's a relationship. I know that I probably hurt your feelings when I walked away from you at the hospital — "

"Try *ran*," she said, but he was on a roll now.

He turned and faced her again, watching her eyes, hoping she was hearing everything he was trying to say. "When I realize that I hurt you, my stomach feels like it's full of glass, and when the thought that you took evidence from a crime scene doesn't even give me a moment's pause because I know it's going to help you do what you want to do, even though—"

"I didn't—"

"I think, maybe, that I'm probably in love with you. And if you don't want me, that's going to hurt like fucking hell, but I had to tell you anyway, because my fucking pride doesn't matter when—"

"Okay. Thanks, Mike. I think it's time for you to go now," she said, and shut the door in his face.

Mike was stunned. He'd thought for a moment there that she was listening to him, that she was considering what he said and thinking about giving him a chance. How had he blown it?

. . .

Lauren faced Alex after she turned her back on the future she might have had. In that moment, she didn't give a damn about the weapon pointed at her. She could have strangled the son of a bitch. How on earth had she ever gone out with him? Why hadn't she seen how greedy he was? How that unbalanced him?

"Good job," Alex told her. "We'll give him a few minutes to get out of the parking lot, and then we'll get out of here."

Lauren was destroyed. Absolutely devastated. The man she loved, the man she wanted to be with more than anyone she'd ever met in her life, had come to her, opened his heart and poured it out for her, and she'd shut the door in his face.

Alex was still talking. "We're going to have to head out of here quickly. Is your gas tank full?"

"What?"

"Do you have a full tank of gas? Because I'm short on cash, and we don't want to use your credit card, because someone will probably trace it, and we don't want that to happen if we can avoid it."

"Alex, shut up," Lauren snapped. "I'll do what you want, but please. Shut the hell up."

Alex's face reddened, and she realized she'd made a misstep, but he only said, "I get it. Your wittle heart is bwoken. Well, you'll get over it. Right now, we need to leave. Get your things."

Lauren didn't have any *things*, just the dirty clothes she'd been wearing earlier, shoved into the Walmart bag she'd taken her new jeans and T-shirt from a while ago. But she obeyed Alex and gathered up the clothes. Walking to the parking lot, every warning she'd ever heard about not getting into a car with a kidnapper screamed at her to find a way to escape, but Alex had a gun pressed into her side, and she guessed that a bullet would pass through her spleen on the way to her heart if he pulled the trigger.

She unlocked the car and opened the driver's side door as Alex moved around to the other side.

"Don't try anything. I can shoot through the car," Alex warned her.

"No, you can't."

Alex whirled, gun waving as Mike stepped from the shadows, carrying a tree limb like it was a baseball bat.

"Back the fuck off, asshole," Alex said, aiming the gun at Mike. "I will kill you."

"You can try. But I don't think you can." Mike took a step closer, raising the branch.

"Mike!" Lauren couldn't help herself from stating the

obvious. "He's got a gun!"

Alex held the pistol higher, and Lauren screamed as she saw his finger tighten on the trigger.

She wasn't sure if it was her scream or something else that made Alex look her way, but his eyes widened just a fraction as the tree limb came into contact with his head at the same time he pulled the trigger. There was no report. Nothing. And then his face went blank as he disappeared completely from view.

Mike bent over him before straightening with the gun in his hand.

"Hi," he said. "I hope you don't mind, but I wanted another chance to plead my case."

"What the hell were you thinking?" Lauren had come around the end of the car and saw that Alex was unconscious—dead? "He had a *gun*!"

Mike held it out to show her. "See this? Safety. It was on."

"But…but…he could have un-safetied it. Or whatever."

He nodded. "I know. But he already screwed up my big scene. I had a few more things to say before you shut the door on me up there."

Lauren's knees wobbled, and Mike put an arm around her as he put the gun in his waistband.

Before the police, sirens blaring, pulled into the parking lot, before Mike dragged Alex in to tie up his own loose ends, he reached out to touch Lauren's chin. Tip her face up. Hold her gaze in his. "A few minutes ago, I said I'm probably in love with you."

"Yeah. You did."

"I think it's more like definitely." He stroked her cheek and smiled. "Screw that. I am, most definitely, in love with you, Lauren Kane."

Epilogue

It was another three hours before Lauren got to be alone with Mike. Alex was in the hospital, suffering a concussion and handcuffed to a bed, under guard. She and Mike had gone to police headquarters to give a statement after the cops had crawled all over the scene. Crawford promised Lauren that Alex wouldn't be going anywhere for a long time, and she felt like she could breathe for the first time in hours. Days, even.

Mike held the door of the Tucker Police Department open for Lauren, and they exited together. He led the way to his truck and opened that door, as well.

He didn't even have his seatbelt on before she crawled across the center console and straddled his lap. One big hand on each side of her waist, heating her body, he stared up at her, a smile playing about his lips. He moved his hands over her, up and down her ribcage, along her hips. He shifted, and she was pretty sure—yep, his body was saying things that his mouth had yet to articulate.

She decided not to wait for him to speak and kissed him.

It was a long, sweet, slow kiss. There was no urgency, and Lauren took her time, showing him how she felt about him. She planned to show him more later, but for now, this would have to do.

After what felt to be about forty-five minutes of lip lock, she finally let Mike come up for air.

"So," she said.

"So."

"I didn't take the algae. I gave it to Chief Crawford."

"I know."

"You do? But you said—"

He put a finger over her lips. "For a while, I did think you took it. Then Crawford told me you turned it in when I gave him my second statement of the day. But it didn't matter."

"It does matter," Lauren said, leaning her forehead against his. "You're a stand-up guy, and I don't want you to think that I'm shady."

"I don't. Even if you had taken it, I know it would be for the right reasons, to see that your drug can get made and help people as soon as possible."

She shrugged. "Maybe. I don't know. It doesn't matter now, though, because I did turn it in. I'm going to call a couple of pharmaceutical companies in the morning and see if I can give them the notes. I won't earn anything for it, not like I would if I had the bugs worked out and could patent the process, but…"

"Yes, you will."

"No, thanks for the vote of confidence, but—"

"You don't understand." He held up her phone. "Have

you checked your email lately?"

"Where did you get that?"

"You dropped it in the parking lot. I haven't had a chance to give it back to you."

She took it from him.

"Check it. I'll wait."

Lauren moved back to her side of the truck and pulled up her email. She read, and then looked up at Mike. "What did you do?"

He smiled. "I don't know much about science, but I did spend a few summers working at Kentucky Jelly. And Miss Emmaline Tucker's son-in-law is my boss."

"Jason is a Tucker?"

"A Tucker-in-law. And he's got some influence. Not to mention the fact that Miss Emmie was my grandmother's best friend."

Lauren's email was from the Tucker University Female Faculty Foundation. She'd been awarded a $100,000 TUFFF grant, available immediately, for the next year. "But I thought Miss Emmaline's grant was for a married biology faculty member. That's why I never applied for it."

Mike nodded. "It was. She wanted to award it to someone to take the pressure off of female faculty who struggle to maintain research funding and have a family. That's what she needed when she was a young scientist. But Jason and I had a talk with her and convinced her to reconsider. Times have changed. No one has applied for that grant in ten years, so the money was just sitting around gathering dusty old interest."

Lauren snorted.

"She agreed to change the rules, to make it available to

any female faculty member—married, or single—as a financial bridge when funding issues crop up."

Lauren had too many things to say, so she went with the easiest. "Thank you."

He was watching her from the corner of his eye, fiddling with his keys. "So…"

God, he was so damned handsome, sitting there with his heart on his sleeve, those eyes, that jaw, that…everything that was Mike Gibson. "Are you asking me to go steady?"

He pulled her into his arms. "Yeah," he said into her neck, sending a shiver to the very core of her. "I'm asking you to be my girl. Or woman. Lauren, I'm just asking you to…be. With me."

Her breath caught in her throat. Less than a week ago, she'd lived in a world of science and fantasies, never imagining a man like Mike could love her.

And honestly, she never imagined *she* could love a man like Mike. Someone who took control when needed and gave it freely. Someone who protected her yet allowed her to make her own decisions. Someone who made her heart thump and her heart sing.

"So…"

She grinned. "Only if you promise not to use your tools on anyone else's plumbing."

It was later—much later, in Mike's bed—when he tucked Lauren's hair behind her ear and said, "About that one-woman plumbing contract."

"Hmmm?" She answered, only half listening. She was idly making swirly patterns in his chest hair.

"I may be retiring my tool belt."

"Huh?" She sat up, looking down at him. He reached up,

distracted by her naked breasts, so to keep him on task, she pulled the sheet over herself. "What are you talking about? I really hope we're switching metaphors, because I'm pretty fond of the way you use that tool."

He nodded, smiling. "Jason's going to have to find someone else to work on his maintenance crew. With the Devil's Dust no longer in circulation, I'm done at Tucker U. But Crawford offered me a position with the Tucker police department."

"That would be so cool!" Lauren grinned. "I'm so glad you're going to be a cop again."

"I'd be a patrol cop. You know, those Kevlar vests make guys look kinda portly."

"Are you sure it's not the donuts?"

He pulled her back down into his arms and kissed her. "I can think of a few ways you can help me work off the donuts."

"Mmmm." She could totally get behind that.

"Mrrrow!" Possum jumped onto the bed, landing with her claws outstretched within centimeters of putting Mike's, uh, exercise program out of commission.

"Damn, cat!" He said, but reached a careful hand out and was allowed to stroke her highness under the chin.

A shadow crossed Lauren's heart, grief over the loss of her own kitty. But then Possum settled down between her and Mike, the cat's rumbling purr soothing away some of the sharper edges.

"You know, it's good you're gonna be hanging around. Possum needs a strong female figure."

"Does that mean you're keeping her? Making that Foster Dad thing into a real adoption?"

"Maybe…"

Lauren got lost in Mike's lazy grin, the beard stubble and bedhead turning her heart around in her chest.

There was something she needed to say still. "Hey, there's something I forgot to mention earlier. It kind of slipped my mind, what with all the chaos."

"Yeah?" He stroked her shoulder, then met her eyes. "Let me have it."

"I'm probably—no, definitely—in love with you, too. In case you weren't sure."

His hand stilled. "I thought you might be. But it's always good to have cold hard proof."

She got up, shooed Possum out of the room, and proved it to him again.

Acknowledgments

What a long, strange trip we've had!

This book was birthed during NaNoWriMo at the Savvy Authors/ Entangled Publishing Bootcamp Smackdown in 2012, and everyone who participated deserves a hand—especially my team, the other Dangerous Divas: Cathy Perkins, Greta Gunselman, Anne Lange, and Camele Warren.

I want to thank Stephen Morgan and Rochelle French for working sooooo patiently with me and whipping this awkward little manuscript into something to celebrate (We finally finished it! YES!). Thanks also to Terese, Nina... all the Ignite people, and everyone at Entangled. What an amazing group. Liz, you make the best Kool-Aid, I can't stop drinking it.

Thanks to my agent, Nicole Resciniti for all the handholding, cheerleading, and guidance as I navigate this crazy business—and to Mary Sue and the Seymour Sibs: We totally rock! Jessica Lemmon, special thanks for hooking me up. The James Taylor you-know-what cloth is your reward.

Mary Baumhoer and Dawn Alexander—you guys kept telling me not to give up. I didn't. Neither should you.

All of my former science teachers, lab coworkers, and research mentors (especially Sarah) deserve a shout-out. Being a Science Geek is the coolest job ever. Okay, maybe being a Science Geek who is also a romance writer is REALLY the coolest.

Mom and Dad: I think it's actually happening! Thanks for believing in me. Mary and John: Next stop, the endcap at Krogers.

And to my favorite husband and the best three kids I ever had: I love you all. Thanks for surviving on take-out and learning to do your own laundry.

About the Author

Teri Anne Stanley writes fun, sexy romance filled with a lot of love, a little angst, and some nekkid parts.

Teri's career has included sex therapy for rats, making posing suits for female body builders, and helping amputee amphibians recover to their full potential. She currently supplements her writing income as a neuroscience research assistant. Along with a variety of teenagers and dogs, she and Mr. Stanley reside just outside of the thriving metropolis of Sugartit, Kentucky, which is—honest to God—between Beaverlick and Rabbit Hash.